GRIMSTONE HANGOVER

A CROFT & WESSON ADVENTURE 2

BRAD MAGNARELLA

Copyright © 2022 by Brad Magnarella

All rights reserved.

No part of this book may be reproduced in any form or by any electronic or mechanical means, including information storage and retrieval systems, without written permission from the author, except for the use of brief quotations in a book review.

Cover design by Deranged Doctor Design

www.bradmagnarella.com

THE PROF CROFT SERIES

PREQUELS
Book of Souls
Siren Call

MAIN SERIES
Demon Moon
Blood Deal
Purge City
Death Mage
Black Luck
Power Game
Druid Bond
Night Rune
Shadow Duel
Shadow Deep
Godly Wars
Angel Doom

SPIN-OFFS
Croft & Tabby
Croft & Wesson

1

Before I had time to drop my suitcase or lean my cane against something in the sheriff's department conference room, James Wesson was swallowing me in a monster hug.

"You made it!"

"Easy, buddy," I wheezed when my toes left the floor. "Watch the potions."

I may have had a slight advantage in height, but the junior wizard outdid me in muscle by a solid twenty pounds, and I grunted as he leaned back with all twenty of them. He set me down, gripped my shoulders, and held me at arm's length.

"My man, Prof Croft," he marveled. "In the *flesh*."

His broad smile radiated from his deep brown face as though he hadn't seen me in a decade. It hadn't been nearly that long, and he was decked out in the same leather cowboy hat, vest, and steel-toed boots as the last time. The look was remarkable, considering he was from the inner city.

"James, I was just out here last month," I said wearily.

Thanks to a full morning of teaching coupled with a harrowing flight from New York City, my fatigue was verging on crankiness. The dearth of decent coffee in my veins didn't help. "But it's good to see you again," I added, managing a smile.

"Hey, that goes double for me, bro. It's been dull as dishwater around here. No offense, Sheriff."

He peered over at the weathered woman in official tans seated at the table.

"None taken," she shot back. "In fact, coming from you, *dull* is good. Could use a lot more of that."

Sheriff Marge Jackson was the law in Grimstone County, Colorado. Despite her short stature and long years, she wore the star on her breast pocket like she owned it. She was also a rarity in law enforcement, not only believing in supernaturals, but understanding the need for expert assistance. She kept that assistance on a tight leash, however, and had raw leather for a tongue when it stepped out of line.

"Now do I need to get you two a room, or can we start already?"

James and I stammered final greetings as we separated and took seats on opposite sides of the table. The potions and spell implements in my trench coat pockets clinked as I scooted my chair in.

"Welcome back," Marge said to me finally. "Though why you'd partner again with this piece of work is beyond me."

James frowned. "Aw, c'mon now. Prof was stoked to come."

"Definitely," I said, too bushed to sound completely convincing.

As wizards went, James was fundamentally sound—in fact, he'd had more formal training than me—but I trumped him on experience. And maturity, I supposed, but only because James set a low bar. Routine jobs he could handle, but the superior members of our magical order wanted me to help out on the more involved cases until he'd earned his stripes. Our last collaboration had been a success, thanks to some lucky breaks. Indeed, teaming up with James always felt like a gamble.

"You're also the reason we're sitting here," Marge added.

"Seriously?" James said. "I was acting in self-defense."

"You *provoked* him."

"Prof was there." He turned to me. "Tell her."

"You provoked him," I said.

His wounded look said, *Really, man? I thought we were a team.* But I didn't have the energy to play favorites.

"James told me his version of events over the phone," I said to Marge, taking out my small notepad and pencil. "Why don't you lay it all out?"

She snorted. "I would've loved to have been a fly on the wall for *that* piece of fantasy, but here's what we've got." She patted a scattering of manila folders beside her. "You met Santana when you were out here last time."

"How could I forget?" I muttered.

The alpha wolf and gangster had nearly done us in, all because James had hustled at one of his pool halls, "forgotten" to pay a commission on his winnings, and then made Santana look weak in front of his pack. Not that Santana was blameless, but to say James had provoked him was putting it nicely.

"Santana operated a couple businesses in the trucking district," Marge continued. "A major drug-running operation too. Yeah, yeah, criminal out the wazoo, but there's only so much I'm equipped to handle." She gestured around to indicate her small department and, by proxy, her small budget.

"He ran grass mostly, some powder, but I made it clear that if he ever started moving that synthetic shit through Grimstone, I'd put his ass in a sling. Got enough problems without our addicts turning into raving lunatics. Santana and I had an understanding there, at least. Then your partner buried a dagger in his guts, and he vanished. His pack scattered, the legit businesses shuttered, and things went quiet. I very nearly congratulated Wesson here—imagine that—but then a new drug showed up this week."

"What kind?" I asked.

With a grave look, she placed her finger on the topmost file folder and slid it toward me. "See for yourself."

I opened the folder to a photo of what looked like a mummified corpse. Hairless gray flesh vacuum-sealed to the bone, wasted nose, yawning mouth. And yet in the pits of the eye sockets, I made out a glistening pair of pupils. I also saw that the victim wasn't on a steel table but a hospital bed.

"He's alive?" I asked in disbelief.

"*Was*," Marge said. "Same with the other three." She nodded at the photos underneath, which I flipped through. "Three guys and a gal, all in their late teens. Thanks to an anonymous call, they were picked up from an abandoned farmhouse, a known drug hangout, and taken to Mercy. By the time they arrived, they were already desiccating. Doctors pumped them full of fluids, but the kids didn't make it to morning. Toxicology found a foreign compound in their systems. A synthetic drug, most likely."

I jotted down the info. "Any idea where it originated?"

"We didn't find anything back at the farmhouse, but it didn't come from Santana, that's for sure." She narrowed her salty blue eyes at James. "Looks like some newcomer stepped into his power vacuum."

"When we crack the case, will you promise to stop putting this on me?" James asked.

Marge sucked her teeth, considering the offer. "We'll see. You can start by telling him what you found."

"Believe it or not, Prof, I've been busting my hump these last couple days. All right, so Marge here scored me a blood sample from one of the vics, and I pulled out all my old alchemy notes from training."

"You took notes?" I asked in surprise.

"Turns out the foreign compound was magically bound," he continued. "It couldn't exist otherwise."

"Good work. Type of magic?"

"Powerful," he said.

"And...?"

He looked guilty as he twirled the silver cross that hung from his neck. "I might've pushed a little too hard and destroyed the sample. Turned out that was my one shot, too. The remaining blood dried up—turned to ash, basically."

"Along with the rest of the vics' bodies," Marge said. "The mortician put them in urns, said they were as good as cremated. Broke my heart to have to inform the parents. Kids might've been delinquent pains in the asses, but they came from decent families." Her gaze turned flinty. "I want you to find this new dealer before he wipes out half my county. And I want him alive. I don't care who or what we're dealing with. We're gonna send a message that we don't stand for that crap in Grimstone."

I nodded. "Any leads?"

"The case info's all in here," she said, pushing the remaining folders toward me. "Plenty to get you started."

I cocked an eyebrow. The last time I'd been out here she had guarded the case file like a bull terrier.

"I won't be around to hold your hands," she explained. "I'm headed to Colorado Springs for business in federal court starting tomorrow morning." She checked her watch. "In fact, I should've left an hour ago. Skull Ridge is no place to be driving through after dark."

James and I exchanged looks of relief, but the feeling didn't last.

"I'll be assigning you Deputy Franks. Wherever you go, he goes, even if it's to the men's room to tinkle. Understood?"

I straightened. "Oh, I assure you that won't be necessary, Sheriff."

She barked a dry laugh. "Think I've forgotten those stunts you pulled last time. The dwarves are only now simmering down."

"No kidding," James put in. "The one time I forgot to detour around Main Street, Taffy charged my Jeep. Got his shoulder into the back guard before I could haul butt out of there. Damn near capsized me."

He meant Tjalf Brunhold, a phenomenally ill-tempered dwarf whom we'd mistaken for the perp last time—and whom James had attacked. That was on top of pissing off Santana, not to mention agreeing to an ill-advised deal with Helga, a matron witch who ran the town's brothel. But those weren't the reasons I was glaring at my partner. His little anecdote wasn't helping our cause. At all.

Before I could convince Marge to drop the oversight, the door to the conference room banged open, and a lanky man in a tan uniform entered. Though I knew him to be well into his thirties, Deputy Franks looked as if he were still wrestling with puberty. His large ears actually flapped as he strutted in.

Marge stood. "Speak of the donkey."

He removed his highway patrolman glasses with a clumsy flourish and announced, "Reporting for duty!"

"Bessie is down with the shingles," she told him, "and Harriet is still in Hawaii, so Deputy Rollie will handle dispatch remotely. If I can get him on the damned phone," she added with a grumble.

Franks nodded importantly. "Yes, Sheriff."

As James and I rose to see Marge off, she held up a pair of fingers. "I'm back in two days." She rotated her fingers until they were leveled at our faces. "I'm counting on you two not to screw this up."

"No, ma'am," we replied in unison.

She smiled tightly, threateningly, and limped from the table on her prosthetic leg. At the door, she stopped. "And take good care of Franks. The minute I get back, we're due in court. No deputy, no case."

"No worries," James said. "He's part of the posse now."

"That's exactly what worries me," she muttered and left.

Despite my feelings about being chaperoned, I greeted Franks properly. He hadn't asked for the assignment, and he had that eighty-pound-weakling look that was hard not to feel sympathy toward. Even so, I got straight to the point.

"How often are you reporting to Marge?"

"On the hour from eight a.m. till midnight and with every major development." He patted the phone in his hip holster. "Oh, and if you guys try to ditch me."

James chuckled. "And why would we do that? Hey, while the prof and I get started on the case file, how about picking us up a couple steak burgers from Pauline's." He pulled a wadded-up bill from his pocket and tossed it to Franks.

"Uh, no can do." He bobbled the bill like a cartoon character. "Line of sight at all times—sheriff's orders. But I'll be happy to request delivery."

Damn. He really did plan on following her directive to the letter.

"Fine," I said. "But before James and I tackle the case file, we need to check out the holding area."

James turned to me. "Holding?"

Franks finally secured the bill and stuffed it into a pocket. "Right this way."

We followed him into a locked room in back with a pen, two cells, and a desk, all empty. Grimstone County had a contract with Centurion United to book inmates at its massive for-profit prison upstate.

I ran my cane along the bars of the closer cell. "This'll do."

Understanding dawned across James's face. "Ahh, a defensive ward."

"And why build one now versus later?" I tested him.

"To give the ward ample time to juice up."

"Precisely."

Deputy Franks looked between us in utter confusion.

"Think it'll hold whatever we're after?" James asked. "I mean, that last thing we faced..."

"I have something special in mind." I gave him my most confident smile. "By the time it's at full strength, our combined powers won't be able to bust it open."

2

I stirred from my sleep to the feeling of something hard mashing the side of my face. The effort to crack my eyelids produced painful bolts in both temples that branched down my body, so I kept them closed.

What in the hell did we get up to last night?

When I swallowed, it was like trying to force down sand. My stomach protested, contracting into a nauseous ball.

Man alive...

I pawed around for my pillow but encountered cold cement.

The room swung in a violent figure-eight as I sat upright and found myself staring at a set of bars. I wasn't in James's double-wide in the canyon. I was in the cell we'd warded in the back of the sheriff's department!

I took quick stock of myself. I was wearing the same shirt and pants I'd arrived in, but my trench coat with all my potions and spell implements was gone, including my mother's emo ball. Gone too were my ring, coin pendant, and wallet. The same was true of my cane, which held my father's sword, my main conduit for magic. The realization generated more bolts between my pounding temples. My shoes were missing as well. Sandspurs studded the ankles of my socks, and I could feel grit between my toes.

I peered out again. Powerful warding magic ran along the bars, distorting the rest of the holding area. With a groan, I recalled the assurance I'd given James regarding my ward's power. He was slumped opposite me, against the back wall.

"Hey," I called in a scratchy voice.

When he didn't respond, I nudged him with a foot.

"Mmph-errmm," he moaned, curling away from the stimulus.

I nudged harder, using my heel like a cudgel. "James. Wake up."

He stretched up the arm that had been hooked across his face and scratched his head. With a severe wince, his eyes cracked open. They rolled from side to side as he straightened, absorbing the scene.

"Is it morning?" he managed, his voice gone to gravel.

But I was too fixated on his face to answer. His lip was split, his right cheek swollen and glistening, and something hot or electric had scored his brow, cutting a deep line into his hair. I motioned around my face to indicate his.

"Are you all right, man?"

"I was about to ask you the same," he said, mirroring my gesture.

A mosaic of stinging, throbbing, and aching seemed to land against my face all at once. I ran a parched tongue over my lips and tasted blood. The front of my shirt was spotted with it, the stained breast pocket torn into a listless flap. When I dragged a hand through my stiff hair, I could have sworn I was being scalped.

"Holy hell," I muttered. "Do I look as bad as I feel?"

"Worse, probably," he said, pawing the top of his head for his missing hat, then feeling for his absent cross pendant.

"Wand?" I asked him. "Wallet?"

He shook his head as he patted his pockets. "No phone, either."

"What happened, exactly?" I struggled to think back. "Were we arrested?"

My thoughts immediately went to Thelonious. A decade earlier, I'd made a pact with a powerful incubus spirit to save my life. The price? Allowing him occasional use of my body for carousing. But as my powers grew, so did my capacity to hold him at bay. Only in those rare instances when I'd exhausted my magic did I become a vessel for Thelonious's visits, which involved total blackouts on my end and a mess to clean up for several days following. It looked as if last night had been one of those instances. I made a mental note to get myself checked out at a health clinic.

"Guess so," James replied.

My mind was already cranking into damage-control mode, but I stopped now. "You don't remember, either?"

"Last thing I remember for sure was polishing off those righteous steak burgers from Pauline's and starting on the case file. Then your nasty foot was prodding me in the ribs. How the hell did we end up in here?"

I searched my memory, the act like swimming my arms through a thick mist. But I only got as far as the burgers and case file too—or rather *sitting down* to the case file. I didn't remember anything in the file itself.

"No idea," I said slowly.

We'd been assigned the case of a powerful dealer. Was it a stretch to think he'd drugged our meal? If so, James and I might have locked ourselves inside the warded cell for protection before blacking out. But before I could share the theory, my more critical faculties kicked in and I shook my head. It didn't explain our stripped-down states nor the sand and spurs covering my socks.

"Let's ask Franks," he said.

"Franks?"

I followed his nod to the metal bench bolted to the floor. Underneath, a figure was wrapped in a Native American blanket. Between the rumbling of the air-conditioning and the ringing in my own ears, the deputy's sputtering snores had failed to register until now. I scooted toward James for a better angle.

"Franks!" we called together.

When he didn't stir, I grabbed the back of his blanket and pulled. He'd wrapped himself inside it like a burrito, but he looked a little too compact. And though he was skin and bones, he slid a little too easily.

I released the blanket and drew away.

"Um, I don't think that's Franks in there," I whispered.

James chuckled, causing himself to wince. "'Course it is. He's just curled up." Before I could stop him, he reached forward and shook the figure vigorously. "Franks, wake your lanky ass up!"

With a growl, the figure flopped toward us. I might or might not have screamed, because peering from the hooded opening in the blanket wasn't the pimply-faced Deputy Franks, but the black-and-white muzzle of a pit bull. It took me another heart-slamming moment to realize it was James's dog.

"Annie!" he cried.

James pulled her onto his lap, where she whimpered

excitedly and tongue-lapped his face. James laughed as he unwrapped her.

"What are you doing here, girl?" he asked. "Huh?"

When she was free of the blanket, she ran around the small enclosure excitedly, her leash rattling after her. On her next pass, she seized the scruff of my shirt and tried to drag me along with her. My stomach roiled as I flailed my arms and legs. She stopped when someone entered the holding area.

"Croft! Wesson!"

The portly man who came rushing into view was Deputy Rollie. He was the one Marge had said would be covering dispatch. I'd worked with Rollie—whom James referred to as *Rolls*—the last time. He seemed like a nice enough guy, but had he been the one to lock us up?

"Where's Franks?" he panted as he arrived at the cell door. His dark mustache, usually combed down in a neat lampshade, was in disarray along with his thinning hair. "Sheriff Jackson has been calling him all morning, and he's not answering. His car's missing, too. I've gone to his house, I've tried his radio..."

Great, so to top it off, we'd lost Franks—the one thing Marge had warned us *not* to do.

I cleared my throat. "When did she last talk to him?"

"Around midnight. That was his final check-in."

"What did Franks tell her?"

"That you guys were getting ready to..." His eyes, which had gone glassy, sharpened suddenly. "Why are you asking? You were with him."

"That's the thing, Rolls," James said. "We don't remember anything."

Rollie's laugh was too shallow to reach his belly. "Is that the best you can do?"

Annie growled up at him.

"It's all right, girl," James murmured. "C'mon, Rolls. Would I lie to you?"

"It's true," I put in. "We have no memory after about eight p.m. We're pretty sure someone drugged us."

Rollie's next laugh sounded closer to a sob. "Well, if half of what's coming in is true, you two are pissing up a rope."

"And what's coming in?" I asked carefully.

"Kidnapping? Grand theft auto? Any of that ring a bell?"

"We did that last night?" James asked, sounding more impressed than bothered. "Damn."

"So you're not gonna tell me where Franks is?" Rollie asked anxiously.

"It's not a question of *won't,* but *can't,*" I insisted. "We honestly don't remember."

Rollie scrubbed a hand through his hair. "I was responsible for tracking his phone last night, and I fell asleep. Thing is, the sheriff asked me last minute, and I was already four beers into happy hour—can you blame me for getting groggy? Now I can't get his signal." When he consulted his phone again, I thought he was going to break down.

"Marge assigned our chaperone a chaperone?" James said. "Man, that woman's got trust issues."

But Rollie getting the assignment—and blowing it—was a positive. If he was as afraid of Marge as we were, chances were good he hadn't told her about Franks going missing or the trouble we'd gotten into last night.

"Does she know about this?" I asked, gesturing around.

"Not yet," he said, cementing my theory. "I need to be able to tell her something good."

Catching on, James went full-court press. "Damn right you do. When Marge learns you lost Franks, she'll go apeshit. Then good luck finding another job in this county. You've got a family to support, right?"

Rollie's eyes went glassy again.

We had him. Now it was time to offer ourselves as the solution. "Let us out, and we'll backtrack," I said. "We'll fix whatever mess we made, find Franks, and get the investigation going again."

James nodded earnestly. "By the time you talk to Marge, it'll be good news all around. We'll even throw some major cred your way."

"B-but you broke the law," he stammered. "And Sheriff Jackson has a zero-tolerance policy. I can't just let you—"

"Yeah, we've seen her billboards," James cut in. "The thing to remember, Rolls, is that we *allegedly* broke the law. Think about it—new dealer in town, a couple crack wizards on the case. Next thing you know, we're drugged out of our minds and being accused of this and that. Sounds like a setup to me."

"It is a little too convenient," I agreed. "And while we're locked in here, the perpetrator is out there, free to kill again."

Rollie's eyes shifted between us apprehensively.

"See that glowing symbol beside the lock," I said, angling my eyes down. "Just press your thumb against it, make a star pattern twice, and pull."

It was the ward's outer release. Rollie started to reach for the sigil, then hesitated. I could see the conflict in his eyes: Go double or nothing, as we were urging him, or own the loss and face the consequences.

"Rolls, baby," James said softly. "It's us. Your buds."

We were both standing in front of him now, trying to

appear as harmless as possible despite our wild hair, stained clothes, and busted-up faces. With the sigil's magic glowing against the deputy's arriving thumb, James grinned, revealing a top row of teeth lined with blood. Rollie snatched his hand back.

"I-I'm gonna go look for Franks," he stammered.

"Wait!" we shouted as he hurried from the room. Annie contributed to our pleas with barking.

Moments later, an engine revved up, wheels spun gravel, and then both faded.

Rollie had officially ditched us.

3

James looked the bars up and down. "You wanna tell me some more about this *unbreakable* ward you installed?"

"Yeah, yeah, let me think it over," I grumbled.

I began an unsteady stroll around the cell—I always thought better with motion—but by my second turn, I had vertigo. Plus Annie kept getting in the way. I sank onto the bench and focused on a spot on the floor between my socks. Last night, I'd taken a basic defensive ward and bolstered it with two complex sigils—

"How did Rolls even get us in here?" James asked.

"If we were that out of it, he could have dragged us," I replied distractedly.

"Hey, what was that thing you asked him to do?"

"It's a kill switch for the warding," I snapped. "Can you give me like three minutes of quiet so I can think?"

"Wow. Touchy."

I stared at him. "Has it occurred to you the absolute shitshow we're in? We have no idea what happened last night, other than that we committed a string of felonies and lost

Deputy Franks; the minute Rollie loses his nerve he's going to call Marge; there's a killer still on the loose; and we're trapped in here."

"Yeah, about sums it up."

"So I'm sorry if I'm acting too *touchy* for your liking, but I'm trying to figure out how to get us out of here."

"Excuse me for wanting to help."

I exhaled a couple choice words and refocused. Where was I? Right, two sigils. The first was for extra protection against nether beings. But the second, regrettably, was designed to guard against a spectrum of magic, including the parts mine and James's operated in. If I could somehow disable that one...

"Press, two star patterns, and pull," James murmured.

It took me a moment to register what he was saying. By the time I looked up, he was squirming a hand between the bars, reaching for the glowing sigil on the lock.

"No!" I shouted.

A bright flash, and James was airborne, slamming into the concrete wall at the rear of the cell. He landed in a sprawl, smoke curling from the hand he clutched to the chest of his gray T. Annie, who had flinched back, sniffed toward him cautiously. Only when the smoke thinned did I see that he still had his fingers.

"You all right, man?"

"Yeah, fine." He shook the hand, dispersing the rest of the smoke. "I pulled out at the last second."

"Lucky you," I said dryly.

"Have you come up with anything?"

"In the ten seconds before my ward nearly Luke-Skywalkered your hand? No."

"Well, you weren't kidding about the power in that thing." He stood and flexed his fingers. "Who-eee!"

I shifted to my wizard's senses to gauge just how powered-up the ward really was. Concentric lines of energy hummed around the bars—except where James had inserted his hand. There, the pattern was disorganized, allowing in some ley energy. Made sense. The ward hadn't had enough time to achieve full strength yet.

If only we had a decent conduit, I thought, peering around. My gaze locked onto Annie's collar.

"Are those studs silver?" I asked James.

"Well, sterling, but yeah."

"They'll do."

I reached for Annie's studded collar. She'd warmed to me after saving her life the last time, and now she thought I was playing. Ducking away, she barked excitedly, ready for me to give chase.

"Come 'ere, girl," James said. "I can tell the prof just had one of his lightbulb moments."

He removed her collar and handed it over. She leapt for it a couple times before he ordered her away.

"The ward's response to your breach disorganized the defense in that one spot," I explained. "It's temporary, so we'll need to work fast, but if we channel our combined powers into the collar, I think we can take it down."

James laughed. "Were you just flexing when you said our powers wouldn't be able to bust it open?"

"A little," I admitted. "You might want to cover Annie with the blanket."

As James gathered his dog and bundled her back up, I carefully fastened her collar around the bar above the lock.

When we'd both finished, I stood back until James and I were shoulder to shoulder.

"Channel as much into it as you can." I whispered. "When I say, 'let it go,' let it go."

"I don't think the ward can hear you, but all right."

We extended opposite hands toward Annie's collar and began. Immediately, the pressure in the cell dropped. In another moment the collar began to rattle. The ley energy in the cell was scant, so I tapped into the innate energy in my wizard's blood. I hoped James was doing the same. Sweat trickled down my sides and spotted through my shirt.

When I'd channeled everything I could into the clattering collar, I started the countdown with a clenched jaw.

"Three... two... one..."

"Disfare!" we shouted in unison.

4

The energy released with a boom that flattened the two of us. My head rang as James and I untangled ourselves and peered around the deafening post-blast. Annie peeked out from under the blanket. Her collar was still dangling above the lock where I'd fastened it, but the silver studs had blown all over the floor. The adjacent bars were angled out. Similarly, the lines of the wards were helter-skelter.

"Did it work?" James asked.

"We'll know in a sec," I said, rubbing my tailbone as I staggered toward the door.

With no time to lose, I winced and stuck a hand between the bars. The section of ward tried, but it was too disjointed to repel me. My gamble had paid off. I thumbed out the pattern over the sigil, and the lock released. The three of us hurried out, Annie dragging her blanket with her. I retrieved her stud-less collar.

"Hot damn," James muttered, gripping the knees of his jeans.

But I was too preoccupied with the whereabouts of my cane and spell implements, not to mention my suitcase, to feel relief, much less elation. "Where would Rollie have put our personal effects?"

James stood and cocked his head. "This way."

At the evidence room, he felt along the ledge above the door and pulled down a spare key. We entered and began looking through boxes, but within minutes it was clear our stuff wasn't there. Next, we searched the conference room, where our memories of last night had ended. Nothing. I looked over the cleared-off table.

"Any idea what we did with the case file?" I asked.

"I was just wondering the same. Must have taken it with us, wherever we went."

James left to search the rest of the department. In a trashcan, I found greasy balls of foil and three empty drink cups—evidence of our dinner from Pauline's. I dug past them, in case we'd thrown out anything important, but we hadn't. I removed the can's plastic lining and knotted it around the small haul.

"What are you doing?" James asked as he returned.

"If someone drugged our dinner, the evidence will be in the packaging."

He nodded. "Could come in handy if our own cases go to trial," he added casually. "Well, I looked, and our stuff isn't anywhere."

I swore. Aside from needing my stuff to perform effective magic, we were talking about irreplaceable gifts and heirlooms. And though James didn't show it, his wand had sentimental value too, being from his first mentor.

Closing my eyes, I focused on my cane sword, the item to which I was most powerfully connected. But either it was outside my range or my head was too fuzzy, because I wasn't picking up anything.

"There has to be *something* of ours around here," I said.

James nodded at a ceiling-mounted camera. "Too bad those haven't worked in years. Could have at least shown us how we left and came back. But I wouldn't sweat it. We probably dropped our stuff at my place when we got Annie."

"And why would we have done that?"

He shrugged and looked around. "Speaking of Annie, have you seen her?"

When I shook my head, he whistled sharply. A whine sounded from the next room.

We entered the breakroom to find it trashed. Beyond a field of crumpled beer cans, Annie was crouched low, doing something weird with her haunches. She looked from us to the toppled couch and whined again.

While James went over, I lifted one of the beer cans and noted the ring of liquid around the top. These were from last night. I added the can to the rest of the garbage I was toting in the plastic bag.

"What is it, girl?" James asked Annie.

As he knelt beside her, I leaned toward one of the walls, trying to remember if it had looked this banged up the last time I'd been in here. And were those burn marks? When I sniffed one, I picked up a scent of ozone.

James shouted.

I turned in time to see a black rope darting from behind the couch, coming just short of my partner's crotch. Stumbling backward while trying to cover Annie at the same time, he tripped and landed ass down.

"Black mamba!" he stammered, shoving himself with his heels. "Black mamba!"

The rope was indeed a snake, and it looked seriously pissed as it raced toward him and his dog.

"Protezione!" I called.

Energy forked from my extended fingers, forming a crude barrier. The leaping snake slammed into it, but no sooner had it landed, it was darting back and forth, seeking a way around. I tried to enclose it in a sphere of hardened air, but without my implements, my magic lacked precision and I failed repeatedly.

James, meanwhile, had cornered himself. Annie, whom he'd been trying to cover, struggled from his grasp and barked furiously at the snake, which had just found a clear route to them. I seized Annie's blanket from the floor and threw it. The heavy blanket spread over the snake, burying it.

James quickly gathered the blanket around the hissing reptile, enclosing it in the equivalent of a sack. "I have to deal with rattlers that slip in the trailer from time to time," he explained. "But a frigging black mamba? Think someone planted it in here?"

I nodded across the room to where a terrarium-like cage lay on its side with its lid open. "Looks that way."

"Can you grab that?"

"The cage?" I asked, incredulous. "You want to transfer the snake?"

"Hey, it'll be more secure in there than this thing." He gave the blanket-turned-sack a shake, riling up the black mamba.

"Don't you dare drop it."

I brought the cage over while James manipulated the blanket. The snake fell into the terrarium so suddenly that I was almost too slow to slam the screened lid closed. I fastened the latch as the snake's head banged against it.

"Holy hell," I breathed. "A little warning next time?"

"I didn't even know it was coming out. I thought it was somewhere else."

The deadly snake darted around its enclosure, striking toward us. Annie barked at it from a safe distance. Only when the snake settled down did I notice the elastic collar someone had affixed around its neck.

"Well, I've solved the mystery of our footwear," James announced.

I followed his nod to where his boots and my shoes, visibly scuffed, lay on the far side of the couch. That was something, anyway. He tossed me my pair, scattering sand over the floor, and stepped into his boots.

"Hey, my other duds are back here, too." He picked up his cowboy hat, restoring the crushed crown, and grinned as he put it on. "Looks like we were active participants in this little beer fest."

"Any sign of my coat?" I asked, hopefully.

"Nah, just my vest." He checked the pockets, but they were empty.

I brushed sandspurs from my socks before slipping on my shoes and double-knotting the laces. "We need to retrace our steps from last night. Figure out where we went and why."

"Easy. What's the very first thing we would've done?"

"Followed up on something from the case file," I said. "Which we don't have."

"You know... we *could* call Marge. Franks gave the sheriff updates till midnight, so that'd cover our first four hours." He caught my very dubious look. "Hey, I'm just saying it's an option."

"And get run out of town?"

"Oh, she'd do a lot worse than that."

"Then let's make that our final option, when all other options have been exhausted or Marge comes back." I noticed something in his pants pocket. "Hey, what's that?"

"Man, don't be pointing down there."

"Not that," I said, jabbing my finger for emphasis. *"That."*

James looked down at the small lump. He inserted a hand and pulled out a cube of blue chalk for a pool cue.

"Why doesn't that surprise me," I muttered.

"Hey, that wasn't in there when I yanked these pants on yesterday. I swear."

"Hold onto it, then. It's a clue." I searched my own pockets and found a business card in the left front one. I read it aloud. "Gunter Bachmann, MD. Clinical Toxicology. Mercy Hospital.' Seems we visited the hospital last night."

James chuckled. "This is seriously starting to remind me of that movie."

"What movie?"

"C'mon, you know. Those guys go to Vegas for a bachelor party and end up blacking out and losing the groom? Man, I'm totally blanking on the name. It's got that funny little fat dude with the beard?"

"I have no idea what you're talking about, but this is real life." I held up the doctor's card. "Let's go."

"Hold up," James said, rechecking all of his pockets. "I don't have my keys."

"Maybe you left them in the ignition."

"Wouldn't be the first time after a late night," he admitted as he leashed Annie. "Grab the cage."

I stopped. "You seriously want to take along the world's deadliest reptile?"

"You think it's better leaving it in here for someone else to stumble over?"

"Fine," I breathed, lifting the cage. "But it goes in that locked compartment in back."

We made our way through the empty sheriff's department and out the front door. Though the morning was cloudy, the leaden light resurrected my headache and burned my squinting eyes. James pulled the bill of his cowboy hat low as he scanned the lot. "Oh, c'mon. Are you telling me my ride's gone too?"

He was right. His black Jeep was nowhere in sight.

"What about that?" I asked.

He followed my pointed finger to the car parked over a row of bushes. Gaudy purple, the 1970s-era Cadillac had been customized with a massive gold grill, eye-popping headlights, and various chrome additions. A leopard-like pattern adorned the rooftop and what I could see of the interior.

"Oh, hell, no," he said.

"What?" I asked, walking toward it.

"It's a pimpmobile. James Wesson doesn't do pimpmobiles. I've got an image to uphold in this town."

"Well, there are keys inside, and it's our only option, so..."

He looked around as if his Jeep might magically manifest before shaking his head and opening the door.

"This is so wrong."

5

"Are you sure this is the most direct route to the hospital?" I asked.

Outside my window, the houses had petered out and ranch fencing was zipping past. I looked over at James, who was hunkered low over the Cadillac's heart-shaped steering wheel, peering furtively from side to side.

"Just trying to avoid the traffic in town," he said.

"Traffic?" I repeated dryly. "In Grimstone?"

"You'd be surprised."

"You know, it's amazing that with everything going on, you're more concerned about being seen in this car than finding Deputy Franks, undoing the damage from last night, and solving the case."

"I can drive faster out here."

"For all we know, Franks could be in serious trouble."

"Well, what if this ride is stolen? Rolls did mention grand theft auto, and this car doesn't exactly fly under the radar."

"Admit it," I said. "That only now occurred to you."

"Maybe so, but we'll get there in the same amount of time as if we'd gone through town. Just watch."

The engine rose an octave as he pressed the gas.

"At least let your poor dog put her head out the window," I said.

James peered into the rearview mirror. Still worked up from the black mamba—who was safely stowed in the trunk—Annie paced the backseat with an anxious whine. "We're almost there, girl," he told her.

"Unbelievable," I muttered when he left the windows up.

James didn't want to risk being recognized as the pimp-mobile driver by way of his dog. Feeling bad for her, I reached down for the seat lever to give her some more room. Something was in the way, and I fished it out. It was my flip-top notepad, my pencil still nested in the metal spiraling.

"M-my notes!" I stammered.

"No way! What's inside?"

I flipped through the pages until I arrived at the highlights I'd jotted down when Marge was going over the case. I turned the page in anticipation—and my shoulders slumped. Blank. I flipped through the rest of the notepad.

"Don't keep me in suspense, Prof."

"There's no denouement." I showed him the blank pages.

"Doesn't seem like you not to take notes."

"No, it doesn't."

I checked the binding, but it didn't appear that any pages had been ripped out. When I reached the end, I turned the pad around. I'd written something on the final page, as if I'd been in too much of a hurry to open the pad properly.

"'Swan Song,'" I read aloud.

"'Swan Song,'" James repeated, brow furrowed. "What the hell does that mean?"

I mouthed it a couple more times to see if it would jiggle loose a memory. "No idea, but it's new. I wrote it down last night."

I searched the glove compartment and floor for anything else we might have left. Finding nothing, I climbed into the back—much to Annie's delight—where I combed the shag carpeting and felt around the seats. All I discovered was a ragged black feather. Maybe nothing, but I pocketed it anyway. *Might be worth casting a hunting spell on if and when I recover my cane.* I finished up at the same time James swung into the hospital's main lot. He steered the Cadillac onto a rear service drive.

"Gonna park it back here," he said, easing behind a dumpster. "You know, so no one gives Annie trouble."

"How noble of you."

Toxicology was a cluttered lab area in the hospital's basement. We asked around for Dr. Bachmann until an assistant led us to a room of expired chemicals and had us wait on a pair of coolers. A tall man in a stained lab coat entered a few minutes later. He stared at us blandly, eyes bloodshot above his thicket of a beard, as if he'd just awakened from a year-long nap. He yawned and scratched his ample gut.

"You again," he said.

I stood. "We promise not to take up too much of your time, Dr. Bachmann. We just have a few questions."

"You've *already* taken up too much of my time."

I could only imagine what I'd done or said while under the influence of the mysterious drug last night, and there was absolutely no telling with James. I felt our best chance of getting in the doctor's good graces would be for James to do none of the talking. Before that could happen, though, my partner stepped in front of me.

"Bong Man?" James said.

"What are you calling him?" I hissed.

"It *is* the Bong Man!" he exclaimed, doubling down. "I met you at a concert out at Clover Fields a few months ago. I was with those two chicks? We partied till morning, remember?" James turned to me. "This dude is serious royalty."

Dr. Bachmann's chest inflated before he caught himself. "Didn't we have this conversation last night?"

"That's the thing," I said, jumping at the opening. "We have no memory of last night."

"Heh. Doesn't surprise me with this guy." The doctor smirked at James, who beamed.

"That means everything coming from the king. Just so you know, Prof, this was before you came out here last month and straightened me out. I'm clean now. I swear it on the stash in my cellar."

Dr. Bachmann snorted, and James leaned against him, chuckling. Well, we were in the doctor's good graces now.

"So, about those questions," I said.

"Make it fast," Dr. Bachmann grumbled, accepting a fist-bump from James before straightening. "I've got a snake bite victim coming in."

"Black mamba?" James asked.

"Prairie rattler." The doctor looked at him sidelong. "Why?"

"No reason," I interjected. "First, what were we doing here last night?"

"You're serious about having no memory?"

James nodded. "Someone slipped us something funny—and not the good kind of funny. We're thinking it's the same cat who poisoned those kids."

Dr. Bachmann drew a phone from his lab coat and tapped out a message while he talked. "You wanted me to explain the compound I'd discovered in the victims' blood. I told you it would be too complex, and I was right. Even when I dumbed it down, the two of you stared at me like a pair of cows."

I tensed at the insult. "And what time was that?"

"I was just about to get off, so around midnight."

"Was there another guy with us?" I asked. "Tall, lanky, big-eared?"

"You don't have to paint a portrait, Rembrandt. I know Deputy Franks. And, yeah, he was here too."

"Were we acting odd?" James asked.

"Compared to what?" he replied snidely.

I was getting the impression that Dr. Bachmann was *not* someone who needed his ego inflated any further. I hoped James was picking up on that too. The door opened, and his assistant arrived with a loaded tray.

"Jenny's going to take your blood and urine," Dr. Bachmann said. "See what's in your systems."

I should have thought of that, but in my defense, I was still recovering from a complete blackout, a jailbreak, and an encounter with a deadly snake. My head was a hazy jumble of conflicting signals.

The doctor's gaze dropped to the plastic liner in my grasp. "Did you wake up thinking you were a garbage collector?"

I bristled at his smug look and James's fake laugh and cleared my throat. "I brought some food packaging the drug might've come in. Any chance you can test it, too? Might help us find the perp."

The doctor nodded grudgingly, and Jenny took the bag from me.

"Anything else?" He scrubbed his beard, producing a dusting of dandruff over the paunch of his brown shirt.

"Did we happen to say where we were going when we left last night?" I asked.

"Do I look like a stenographer? I did catch you arguing about whether to go to Pauline's Diner before or after going somewhere else. Seems you and Franks outvoted James here, so if you ended up at Pauline's, it was after."

I turned to James. "Again with Pauline's?"

"C'mon, you had their steak burger. They're awesome, right?"

"By the way, who played speed bag with your faces?" Dr. Bachmann asked, then raised a hand. "Oh, right. Forgot. Lost your memories." He snorted. "Featherweights."

"Thanks for your help," I growled.

"Yeah, thanks, Bong Man." James pumped a fist. "All hail the king!"

Dr. Bachmann smirked as he backed toward the door. "Give us till the afternoon on those results. Oh, and Jenny? When you stick them, make sure it hurts."

As the door swung closed, James turned to Jenny, "He's kidding, right?"

Her lips pursed down as she snapped on her gloves.

We exited the hospital, rubbing our sore arms.

"You just had to carry on with that *king* stuff," I said.

"I didn't know it was going to make him act like an asshole."

"That's my point—he was already acting like one."

"Well, if it's any consolation, there's nothing royal about him," James said. "That party I mentioned? He took one bong hit and wouldn't stop crying until he fell asleep in a fetal position. It was weak stuff, too. The nickname was supposed to be ironic. Anyway, what are you complaining about? We got what we came for."

"I could have done without Nurse Ratched ventilating my arm," I muttered.

But James was right. We had further confirmation that Deputy Franks had been with us until midnight; we had a lead on somewhere else we might have gone; and by the end of the day, we would know what we'd been drugged with and possibly how the drug had been delivered. Something was bugging me, though.

"I know that wrinkly-browed look, Prof."

"I'm just trying to figure out what happened between eight p.m. and midnight that would have prompted our interest in the drug's makeup."

"Maybe we were working down a list."

"Or following a lead. I'd love to know where we went right after. That was Franks's final check-in to the sheriff."

"Rolls could tell us," James said. "Hell, he almost let it slip back at the cell."

"I don't think tipping the deputy off to our fugitive status is the best move right now. He's too freaked out. He could decide to call Marge, and the last thing we need is her coming back early."

"She said she'd be gone two nights, right? So that gives us until, what, noon tomorrow?"

"At the very latest," I said. "Why don't we check out Pauline's Diner, see if we made that early morning stop."

James nodded. "Might as well grab a couple burgers while we're there."

I stared at him as we walked down the service drive. "Or maybe we should wait for the toxicology report on the packaging first? Unless you want to forfeit today to memory loss as well, then by all means."

James stopped suddenly and grabbed my arm. For a moment I thought my sarcasm had crossed a line, but he was staring ahead.

"What?" I asked.

"Astral level."

I shifted to my wizard's senses until the humming patterns of astral energy bled into our surroundings. Now, a cloud of dark smoke was visible above the dumpster we'd parked behind. James and I side-stepped over for a better view.

"Crap," I muttered.

A party of scrawny, pigeon-sized creatures were zipping around the Cadillac, their ragged wings kicking up smoke. Imps. And not just any imps, which I despised enough, but ones I recognized as servants of Helga, the town's matron witch.

Some of them were jumping up and down on the rooftop, while others played with the wipers. One of the larger imps succeeded in pulling out the antenna and began whipping another imp with it. But most were taunting Annie through the glass.

Dogs possessed astral acuity, and James's was no exception. Plus, these particular imps straddled the physical world. Annie barked furiously and smashed her thick head against the window trying to get at them.

That only made the imps egg her on more.

"Oh, hell, no," James said, stalking forward.

"Wait," I hissed. *"They're Madam Helga's."*

"And they're messing with the wrong wizard's dog."

With silver energy crackling around his fists, he broke into a charge.

6

"Leave her alone!" James shouted.

I'd run up to try to talk my partner back down, but I was too late. The imps turned their grins and stick-like noses from the car. At the sight of James incoming, their harsh cackles changed, rising into a collective screech that sounded like a war cry. In a storm of smoke and batting wings, they flew at him.

Correction: at *us*.

"Wonderful," I muttered.

The silver charge that had been building around James's fist released as a crackling cannonball. It tore through the arriving imps, flattening several and knocking others into dizzying pirouettes, but most of them darted around the assault. Before I could summon an effective shield, they were all over us.

I swore and waved my arms around as small hands yanked my hair, squeezed my nose, and pummeled my ribs. Imps tended to be more annoying than dangerous, but like with most pests, a riled-up swarm could do damage. And thanks to the wounds I'd suffered last night, their attack was already starting to hurt.

"Respingere!" I bellowed.

Energy discharged from my body, scattering the imps. But like pesky flies, they amassed again and returned to work. Damn. That invocation was much more effective with my staff.

"Back!" I shouted, pushing power into my wizard's voice. "Get away!"

The words were too frantic to be effective, however. And amid the swirling storm of impish voices, I started to pick up a common theme.

"Where is he?" "What did you do to him?"

"Franks? I don't know!" I shouted. "We're looking for him too!"

What they would want with the deputy, I had no idea. I was just saying anything to get these maddening things off us. For his part, James remained determined to punish them for provoking his dog. Silver energy seared the air, the harsh scent of ozone clashing with the imps' sulfur. But his efforts were little more effective than mine.

"Get in the car!" I called. "Let's just get out of here!"

At top speed, we could outrace them. I was moving toward the Cadillac in a crouch, swiping at the imps divebombing my face, when something whacked me sharply across the back. I winced around to see the large imp who'd snatched the car antenna smiling stupidly and brandishing it like a whip.

"Hey! What are you—?"

He brought it down again. *Whack!*

I thrust a hand at him. *"Vigore!"*

For a larger-than-average imp, he moved deftly, slipping

around the main lines of force that shot from my palm. Before I could react, the antenna was flashing across my face. The fire that seared my cheek stoked my anger into a wrath. I lunged for him, grasped air, and caught a whack across the knuckles.

"Get over here, you little *shit*," I seethed.

"No, Annie!" James called. "Get back in!"

In the next moment, the imps around me scattered. I peered up to find Annie arriving like a cruise missile. Imps zipped from her snapping teeth, but the big one, who was contemplating where to strike me next, never saw her coming. She seized him in her frothing jaw and shook him violently.

"Help!" he shrieked. "Hel-umph-rmph!"

Several imps circled back and grabbed Annie's ears, but by the time she dropped the large imp to pursue them, he was a crumpled, smoke-leaking wreck. I snatched the antenna from his limp grasp, whipped it around a few times to give myself space, then bent it back and forth in the middle until it snapped.

"James!" I called. "Catch!"

He looked up from his attempt to corral Annie, and I tossed him the antenna's top half. He snatched it out of the air and obliterated an imp into smoke with a silver bolt. I brandished my own half of the antenna in search of a target. An imp nominated himself by swooping in and taking a cheap shot at the family jewels.

"Entrapolare!" I cried.

The energy that swelled from the antenna hardened the air around him into an orb. The imp repurposed his fists in an attempt to break from his confinement, but I was already upping the pressure. He stopped and stared at me, eyes bulging as if in an exaggerated show of disbelief, then burst into a puff of smoke.

One less pest in the world.

James, meanwhile, was sending spiraling bolts down his antenna-wand, eliminating one imp after another like a bug zapper. I squeezed two more imps from existence before the rest understood the tide had turned. They fled en masse. Annie chased them for a short distance before returning to us.

"You all right, girl?" James asked, inspecting a small knot on her forehead.

She panted excitedly, looking around to see if any were coming back, before barking and licking James's hand.

"There were better ways to handle that," I said.

I expected pushback, but James nodded as he retrieved his cowboy hat from the pavement. "I flipped out a little, but Annie's my baby."

"At least we got some temporary casting implements out of it." I looked my half-antenna over, impressed with how well it had channeled energy. I'd have to remember that trick in future pinches.

"You said the imps were Madam Helga's?" he asked.

"Yeah, I recognized a few of them from her place last month."

"How would they have even found us?"

"The witch does have her 'Eye of Baba,'" I said.

"Hold on a sec. Do you think she's involved in the drug case?"

"Hard to say. I'm not sure you heard the imps, but they were asking where someone was. Deputy Franks, I assumed, but it could have been anyone. I just hope we didn't get into something with them last night."

"No kidding. I do not want to have to deal with that broad again."

I almost reminded him of the deal he'd made with Madam Helga—agreeing to complete a task of her choosing—but we already had enough to worry about. Before getting into the car, I paused to see if I'd dropped anything during the melee. Near the dumpster, I spotted something.

"Hey, is that your phone?"

"Holy crap, it is!" James hustled over to it. "Everything we need to know could be on here." But as he stooped to retrieve it, his expression fell. He held it up and showed me the screen—completely smashed.

"Can we replace it?" I asked. "Get it fixed somewhere in town?"

"This model doesn't exist in the States. I got it from a manufacturer out of Ghana, complete with a hacked plan, so I can't transfer the data either. Damn. It was one of the few phones that handled my magic."

Inside the car, he fussed with the phone some more, finally getting it to turn on. It whistled out a very broken-sounding version of "The Good, the Bad, and the Ugly."

"How did the imps get their hands on it in the first place?" he grumbled.

"We must've encountered them last night."

"Well, they're gonna owe me a new phone."

"Does *anything* on it work?"

"Pretty hard to tell with this busted screen. Hold up, there's supposed to be a certain feature…" He pressed a thin button with his fingernail, and a small keyboard released from the bottom of the phone. "Yes! For some reason they built a backup keypad into the model. I can check my voicemail now."

He pressed a button and held the phone to his ear.

"Six messages," he said, then frowned and listened.

Who? I mouthed, turning up a hand. But he held up a finger for me to wait.

A couple minutes later, he sighed and brought the phone down. "Guess how many of those were Marge?"

"All of them?"

"All but one, and that's just some strange dude saying 'yes.' Man, Marge is breathing some serious fire. She thinks we're ghosting her. Said if we're not in the hospital or actual ghosts, our 'asses are grass,' and that's a direct quote. She left the last message while we were talking to Bong Man."

"Did she mention Deputy Franks?"

"Yeah. She's convinced he's in on whatever we're up to."

"So midnight *was* his last check in," I said grimly, "meaning he's been AWOL going on ten hours."

"Should we just come clean?"

I snorted. "Marge is a lot of things, but reasonable is not one of them."

"All right, but if she's calling this many times, I don't think she's gonna stay away another night. Whenever she finishes up in court this afternoon, she's coming back, even if it means driving through Skull Ridge after dark. Unless, of course, we can assure her that everything's under control."

"Is it, though?" I asked dryly.

"'Course not, but I'm a seasoned bullshitter."

"Yeah, and Marge has a supernatural bullshit detector, which makes her the worst possible opponent."

"But if you and me put our heads together—"

"We end up with no memory of the night before, apparently. But if we haven't found Franks by this afternoon, we're going to have to figure something out... and that could involve calling Marge," I conceded.

"If Rolls doesn't call her first."

Crap. I'd almost forgotten about Deputy Rollie.

"Welp..." James cranked up the engine. "Might as well head to Pauline's."

"For information," I stressed. "Not burgers."

7

"Yeah, you two were here," Charlie snarled. "Came in whooping like a pack of loons. Then Jack Johnson here put away his weight in steak burgers." He nodded at James, who made a puzzled face at the antiquated boxing reference. "All that meat-flipping set off the arthritis in my wrist. Had to pop an extra codeine."

Of the staff who'd been at Pauline's the night before, the cook was the only one working today's lunch shift. A pugnacious old man with a hearing aid the size of a Rubix Cube, Charlie's surly expression suggested a wish to be forty years younger so he could kick some sense into us. The surliness had only deepened after we explained that we'd lost our memories. I didn't take it personally—I sensed some goblin in him. He only agreed to talk because it gave him an excuse to take a smoke break out back.

"Do you remember what time?" I asked.

He shrugged. "Two a.m.? Somewheres in there."

"Did we say where we'd been?" James asked hopefully.

"You think I could hear anything working the grill with

this monstrosity." He slapped his hearing aid and took a drag from his crumpled cigarette. "Just sounded like a bunch of happy-ass ruckus to me."

"Did you happen to see how many of us there were?" I pressed.

"Yeah, you two and a beanpole in uniform. Must've been that Franks boy. Eyesight's not too sharp these days, neither."

I was preparing to ask about the condition of our faces—if they'd looked beaten-up yet—but his last remark killed it. The Franks part had me exhaling a small sigh of relief, though. It wasn't necessarily good news, but it shrank the window on his disappearance. The less time he was missing, the less opportunity there would've been for badness to befall him. That was what I was telling myself, anyway.

"I don't guess you heard where we were going?" I asked.

He tapped his hearing aid and glared at me as if to say, "Didn't I just explain this to you, you dumb ox?" He took another drag and squinted into the garbage-strewn ravine that ran behind the restaurant.

James showed me his cube of cue chalk. "There's still this."

"How many pool halls are in Grimstone?" I asked him.

"Half a dozen."

"Which ones do you frequent?"

James shrugged. "All of them?"

"That could take us the rest of the day."

"Let's head back to my place, then. We obviously stopped by last night to get Annie. Might've left behind some clues."

I was nodding when Charlie stamped out his cigarette. "You could always ask Loretta where you went."

I wheeled back toward him. "Who's that?"

"Waitress. She was finishing her shift and left with you guys."

"Damn," James marveled quietly. "Even blacked out, I've got game."

"Do you happen to know where she lives?" I asked.

"Mesa Park Apartments, on the southside," Charlie barked. "Don't know the number, but it's a corner unit on the second level. She hosted the staff Christmas party a couple years back."

"Fantastic," I said. "You've been a huge help."

He grunted and shoved aside the cinderblock propping the rear door of the restaurant. James caught the door and produced a twenty.

"Hey, uh, think you could bag us a couple steak burgers to go?"

"I'm not a damned cashier," he snarled. "Order up front."

"You can keep the change."

Charlie snatched the bill. "I'll have 'em for you in ten."

"Really?" I said to James when the door closed. "Didn't we talk about this?"

"Hey, if I ate my weight in burgers last night, and you and I suffered the exact same effects, the drug clearly wasn't planted in the food."

Damn. He had me there.

Mesa Park Apartments was a two-level building that looked like it had been a motel once. James pulled into a dirt drive that ran along the side of the building and parked behind a cluster of scrub oak. He took down his final bite of burger, wiped his mouth, and checked his face in the rearview mirror for stray condiments.

"Mind grabbing the snake while I get Annie?" he asked, releasing the trunk.

"Do you really think we should show up at her door with a pit bull and a black mamba?"

"Well, we can't leave them in the car."

"Why not?"

"For real? It might've been cool this morning, but we're in a desert climate in summer. In another hour it'll be ninety, and you can add twenty degrees to any parked vehicle. By the time we get back, Annie will've heat-stroked, and the snake will be baked to a crisp. I'm surprised you don't know this."

"I live in a Mid-Atlantic climate," I said lamely.

I got out, slipped my antenna-wand into a back pocket, and lifted the cage from the trunk. As the snake began exploring up and down the plastic walls, I checked to make sure the lid was securely fastened.

"How's our friend look?" James asked as he led Annie from the backseat.

I held the cage up. "Like it would still be very happy to pump us both full of venom."

He chuckled. "It's got attitude, that's for sure." As we crossed the dusty lot, he tilted back his cowboy hat and squinted at the apartment building. "Wonder where we went with this Loretta last night."

"No idea. I just hope she doesn't turn out to be missing, too."

"Oh, c'mon, Prof. Doesn't the thought of us trying to have some fun make you smile just a little?"

"Honestly? No. But I've been thinking about something that might *actually* help our case."

"All right, let's hear it."

"It seemed we had our wits about us at the hospital last night. If we hadn't, Dr. Bachmann would've had no qualms about saying so. But come two a.m. we're acting like fools at Pauline's. I think whatever we were slipped happened during that two-hour window and the memory loss was retroactive."

But James was showing me a hand. "Shush a minute. That old cook said second floor, corner unit, right?"

I tensed my jaw in irritation but followed his nod to where a pair of young women were leaving a unit at the far end of the complex. James's lips forked into a devilish grin.

"Looks like we ended up with a two-fer," he whispered. "A sizzling *hot* two-fer."

Before I could restrain him, he took off toward the stairs and jerked his head. "Keep up, Prof."

I tried, if only to be in position for the inevitable damage control, but the cage was swinging awkwardly in my grip and I didn't want the lid to pop open. By the time I arrived at the top of the stairs, James had already removed his hat and was bowing to the pretty women, who'd stopped in front of him.

"I hope you didn't think I'd forgotten you, Loretta," James said, trying to cover for our complete memory loss.

"Wrong female," the blonde, who was closer, replied.

"No, I meant her." James nodded at the brunette.

She snorted. "You're oh-for-two, buddy. Loretta lives over there."

I would have given anything to have captured James's expression as he followed her nod to the opposite corner unit. It was the perfect mix of crestfallen and *I just made an ass of myself, didn't I?*

"Oh," he said, replacing his hat.

"If that's all, Darius Rucker. We'd like to leave now."

"O-Of course," he stammered, stepping aside for them to pass.

"Wow," I said. "From 'two-fer' to 'oh-for-two.' Now *that* made me smile."

"C'mon, Croft, you were thinking the same thing as me."

"Not nearly in as much detail, I assure you. Anyway, I'm spoken for."

"Oh, yeah?" His face brightened. "With what's-her-name back in New York?"

"Yes, and it's going well with what's-her-name, so let's hope we didn't do anything last night to destroy that. Whatever happened with Allison, anyway?"

His head tilted in question.

"The young woman we saved last time?" I prompted. "Who you swore up and down was the One?"

"Oh!" He snapped his fingers. "You mean Lise. That's what everyone calls her. Yeah, man, things were great until she moved. Decided to go live with her mother in Florida. After what she went through, can't say I blame her."

"Yeah, being a sacrificial offering will do that," I quipped, but when I caught a flicker of hurt in his eyes, I stopped. "Hey, I'm sorry."

He shrugged. "No worries. I'm dealing."

"There you are!" a new voice exclaimed.

We wheeled simultaneously and took in a familiar figure standing in the door of the opposite corner unit.

"Oh, crap," James muttered.

"Crap," I agreed.

The woman with a mass of dark, gray-rooted hair may not have been in uniform, but I recognized her from our run-in at Pauline's Diner a month earlier. James and I had gone there to intercept the killer's next victim. One thing led to another, and the waitress believed we were the culprits. She smashed a pitcher of tea over James's head, sicced a pair of truckers on us, then threatened us with a steak knife. The twist? Violence excited her, and she demanded we take her with us. Total freak, in other words. And yet, she'd apparently gotten her wish in the wee hours this morning.

She was wearing a scarlet robe over a matching negligee, her wide hips pushing the robe from side to side like a sail as she started toward us. I narrowed my eyes at James.

"Hey, you don't know it was me who invited her," he whispered.

"Sure, because I'm the one who's always trying to pick up women."

"I'm just saying you should hold off judgment until we know the whole story."

I realized that if we were going to piece last night together and recover Franks, we *would* need the whole story. Resisting the urge to back away, I reconfigured my lips into a smile. "Just play along," I whispered.

James nodded and fixed a smile on his own face.

Loretta's yellow incisors flared out as she smiled back and hand-signed a beating heart against her chest.

"To a point," I amended from the side of my mouth.

"'To a point' is goddamned right. Even I have my limits when it comes to crazy."

Arriving in front of James, Loretta hooked her fingers through the belt loops of his jeans and yanked him toward her. "Where did you run off to, you bad boy?"

He stammered. "I, uh—"

"I left to get my paycheck from the diner," she said, "and when I came back, you'd gone bye-bye." She lunged up to kiss him. He angled his face toward me at the last moment, and her lips mashed against his cheek. She remained there for several seconds, murmuring as if enjoying a delectable meal.

I smirked. *Hold off on judgment until we know the whole story, huh?*

The anguish in his eyes only heightened my satisfaction at having been right. Loretta released him suddenly and turned toward me. I instinctively moved the snake cage to my front to use as a barrier or possible weapon.

"My baby!" she exclaimed.

Huh?

She was looking down at the cage. I placed it in her grasping hands, then winced as she planted little tongue-kisses where the mamba was flicking its own tongue. That solved the mystery of the snake.

"How you doing, Benny?" she asked in baby-talk. "Hmm? Did you spend the morning with your daddies?"

My stomach drew into a sick knot. "I-I'm sorry. Did you say 'daddies'?"

She laughed until she began to snort. "You two were pretty hammered last night, but you don't remember?"

"Remember what?" James and I asked together.

"The three of us got married!"

8

Loretta invited us into her apartment, saying her snake was overdue his feeding. With our minds blown, and needing more information about last night—*a lot* more information—James and I followed, my antenna-wand in hand.

"Do you like it?" she asked when she caught me peering around.

The walls and just about every available surface area of her living room was covered with yard-sale tat. There was just enough organization to spare her hoarder status, but it was a thin line.

"It's... interesting," I replied. "Very, you know, all over the place."

"I got it all off dead people."

"I-I'm sorry?"

Her eyes shone with pride. "You know, estate sales and such." She lowered her voice. "But I've also got a contact over at King Pawn. He lets me know if someone's bringing in dead-people stuff."

"Lucky you," I said.

"Well, go on and sit down while I grab Benny's lunch." She disappeared into another room. "Can I bring my hubbies some coffee?"

"Black, two sugars," James called.

"Evy-poo?" she asked me.

"No, I'm good." As a microwave roared to life, I turned to James. "You can stop treating her like your wife."

"*Our* wife," he corrected me.

"Speak for yourself. I can't wait to hear how you got us into this."

He lowered himself beside me on the loveseat and ordered Annie under the coffee table, where Loretta had set the snake cage. "Hey, when it comes to polygamy, it takes at least *three* to tango."

I shook my head. "There's no way I went along with that."

"How do you know? We've both got black holes for memories."

"Because I know myself, and I know you."

"That's harsh, Prof."

"And you were the first one she kissed."

"Yeah, because you were hiding behind her snake like a little bitch."

"Let's just learn what we can and get out of here," I sighed. "There's no way that whatever happened is legally binding."

James squinted toward the ceiling, then swore quietly.

"What?" I asked.

"I almost had the name of that movie this reminds me of."

Loretta returned shortly, fisting two coffee mugs in one hand and a squirming white mouse in the other. She extended the mouse toward us before snorting at her own joke and handing us each a steaming mug.

"I brought you one anyway," she said to me with a wink.

I smiled tightly and set my lipstick-stained mug to one side. James took a sip from his and cupped it contentedly on his lap. Loretta dropped the mouse in the snake cage and watched, mesmerized.

"So, Loretta," I began, "we have a couple questions for you."

"Fire away, hon," she said, not moving her eyes from the cage and the mouse's mad attempts to scramble up its slick walls. When the black mamba swung toward it, she giggled in anticipation.

"After we left the diner, where did we go?"

"To James's place," she said distractedly. "Needed to take his baby out for a pee-pee. She was sad to see us go, so he took her along. Wait, watch this—watch!"

The snake struck, seizing the mouse in his fangs.

"Yes, Benny!" she cried. "Pump that poison! Kill it! Kill it!"

She was hunkered in front of the cage now, eyes blazing with blood lust. I scooted back on the couch. Even James crossed his legs. Loretta's cries rose to banshee-like shrieks until the mouse's kicks slowed to twitches. She watched another moment, as if to ensure the struggle was over, before straightening and pushing the terrarium aside.

"The swallowing part can take more than an hour," she said in a deflating voice. "Then I don't get to feed him for another three days." The final glimmer of enthusiasm left her eyes. "Sometimes I think about opening his stomach, taking the mouse out, and sewing the incision closed, just so I can feed him again."

"That would be a bad idea," I said.

James chuckled nervously. "Wow, wild. So, about last night... Deputy Franks was with us, right?"

"Of course. He was part of the ceremony."

Before I could object, James showed me a hand. "And did Deputy Franks drop out at any point? Say he was going somewhere?"

"He was still at the party when I left."

"Party?" I asked.

"Yeah, at the sheriff's department."

I thought about the trashed breakroom and field of beer cans.

"And what time did you leave?" James asked.

"Around five this morning. I had to run back to the diner to pick up my check. Forgot it last night, and you *never* leave your check in the staff room—not unless you want Charlie picking your locker and pocketing it. Anyway, Leslie talked me into helping out with the pre-dawn rush. By the time I got back, you guys were gone. I thought you'd ditched me, but here you are! Guess I can give these back."

She held out a pair of leather wallets.

"You lifted them off us?" I snatched mine from her and searched through it to ensure all of my cash and cards were still inside. James pocketed his own wallet nonchalantly.

Loretta's eyes widened. "What's the fat fuss? I only took them as insurance."

"Oh, gee, did you happen to take anything else? " I asked. "My coat or cane, maybe? His wand?"

"The better question," James said, playing peacemaker, "is did we have those on us in the first place?"

Loretta made a thinking face as she looked me over. "You had a trench coat on. I remember, 'cause I thought it made you look tasty, especially with the top of your shirt open. Don't remember a cane, though. And did you say 'wand'?" she asked James. "As in *abracadabra*? Nah, but don't worry—

I've got closets full of stuff like that, not to mention a big storage unit off Route 70. Now that we're married, what's mine is yours!"

"Listen," I said curtly. "We don't remember anything that happened last night. Besides, polygamy is illegal here. I'm sorry to rain on your reception, but there was no marriage. Now, we'd appreciate it if you could talk us through the timeline from leaving the diner until the party at the sheriff's department."

She snorted a laugh. "That's what James kept saying, but you insisted. You're so danged hard-headed."

I looked up from my notepad. "What did James keep saying?"

"That polygamy was illegal. But you insisted there were ways around it."

"*I* insisted?" I asked. "Me, specifically?"

She brayed laughter, thinking I was putting her on. James smirked as he leaned back and took a sip of his coffee. "Well, isn't this interesting."

"Oh, yeah," Loretta continued. "You said that there were mystical ceremonies that replaced the law if done proper. Jam-jam here didn't believe you—said you were full of dung—but you said you could prove it. Guess I was just the right gal in the right place at the right time." She beamed. "But golly, y'all are competitive. We're gonna have to lay some ground rules before you two kill each other. Not that the idea doesn't work me up a little." She bit her lower lip, a sadistic gleam in her eyes.

I groaned inwardly. Blacked out or not, I hadn't been wrong in my argument. There were ancient ceremonies of matrimony that were considerably more powerful than their legal counterparts.

"And we did the marriage?" I asked to be sure. "We actually went through with it?"

"In the handicapped stall at Chasers. See?" When she held up her left hand, I almost choked at the sight of my grandfather's ring on her fourth finger. She stroked the embossed ingot. "I do love dragons."

"Can I see that?" I asked.

She glanced at James, who nodded it was okay, then splayed her hand toward me. I touched the ring, already not liking the energy encircling it. Though loose on her finger, the ring wouldn't budge when I pulled it. Magically bound. But given how out of it I must've been, how powerful could it be?

I hovered my antenna-wand over the ring and uttered, "*Disfare.*"

Light flashed from the ring, sending my makeshift wand flipping across the room.

"What's the verdict?" James asked when it clattered to a rest.

"Complicated," I muttered, still reeling with the idea that *I'd* been responsible for this. "Really complicated."

"Spell it out."

"Soul binding. Until it's dispelled, we can't have relations with anyone but her."

He glanced at Loretta, who was momentarily lost in wild-eyed admiration for the ring. "Dispel it," he ordered me.

"I imagine most three-way marriages are complicated," Loretta said, standing. "But we'll make it work. We got this far, didn't we? Can I get my hubbies some more coffee, or are you ready for something more filling?" She opened her robe and shifted her negligee-clad hips from side to side in a clumsy dance.

James and I winced.

"Ah, Loretta, we have to talk about something very serious," I said.

"If it's about scheduling time with me, I've already got that part figured out."

"No, no, it's not that," I said quickly. "We're going to need your consent to annul last night's ceremony."

"Annul?" She stopped swaying and planted her fists against the sides of her hips. "Marrying you two was the best thing that's ever happened to me! If you think I'm gonna give that up, you're out of your minds!"

"That's sort of the point," I said. "We *were* out of our minds."

"Loretta, baby," James tried in a soothing voice. "Just listen to what he's—"

He was interrupted by an explosion of splintered wood. The door to the apartment burst open and a group of armed men stormed in.

9

The arriving men were dressed in street clothes and bearing small, box-shaped machine guns. I felt around for my antenna-wand before remembering my own magic had just flipped it across the room.

"On the floor!" they shouted. "Get on the floor!"

I didn't know whether James had grabbed his half of the antenna from the car, but he was showing his empty hands. When our eyes met, his face said, *They're armed, and we're outnumbered.*

Attempt a shield? My earlier effort had been dismal without my cane. As the men swarmed around us, I raised my own hands. What now? One of them grabbed the scruff of my shirt and forced me to the floor. Despite his bony-looking frame, he was strong. His knob of a knee landed in the center of my back.

"Who are you?" I grunted as my wrists were wrenched and bound behind me. More hands patted me down. "What do you want?"

I couldn't tell whether they heard me. Loretta was

shrieking above the commotion—and landing a few slaps, from the sounds of it. She complained as she staggered back and hit the floor, shaking the unit.

"Hey, watch it!" James shouted. "That's our wife!"

"Not our wife," I amended, "but she has nothing to do with whatever this is!"

"Dammit!" one of the men cried. "Let go!"

I twisted my neck around. Annie had lunged from under the coffee table and seized a man's ankle in her muzzle. I winced as gun barrels pivoted toward her head.

"Don't shoot!" James shouted. "Please! Back, Annie! Back!"

I braced for an explosion, but Annie released him and whimpered at James, as if asking him what she was supposed to do.

"You just want my partner and me, right?" James said. "Loretta, hon. Take Annie to the back."

"Do what he says!" one of the men barked at her as a musty sack went over my head.

I was lifted roughly to my feet and forced toward the door. I could hear James staggering behind me, apartment decor spilling in our wake. Outside, the sun and heat hit me like a wall, underscoring James's claim about the desert climate.

"Are you going to hurt them?" Loretta asked, a note of excitement climbing her voice.

"Back inside, freak," one of the men ordered. "Before we decide to hurt *you*."

"You would, wouldn't you?" she said hopefully.

As the men perp-walked us down the stairs, Loretta called, "Don't worry, darlings, I'll wait for you! I'll be faithful!"

Well, that's reassuring, I thought.

I ended up in the backseat of a vehicle, an armed man pressed to either side of me. Were they connected to the drug case, or just another rude surprise from the night before? Could explain our beaten-up faces.

As we pulled from the lot and picked up speed, I tried to tell them about our lost memories—in the event we *had* run into them last night—but was cut off with a sharp warning to shut up or get shot.

"I'll shut up," I said.

I clamped my tongue but opened my wizard's senses. The men had looked odd, with their stooped upper backs and bony limbs. Now their auras were telling me they weren't entirely human. Shifters? Possibly, but it wasn't like any shifter energy I'd encountered before. I sniffed the air. Vaguely rotten.

Sometime later, we pulled off the asphalt and onto a bumpy road. It smoothed shortly, and the doors on either side of me opened. The men pulled me out into a cool space. James arrived beside me.

"You all right?" I whispered.

"Took some knuckles to the ribs for asking questions. You?"

"I only got yelled at. I'm just really confused about what's going on."

"Well, whatever's happening, don't be putting it on me this time."

"Lesson learned," I said.

When the sacks were yanked from our heads, I saw we were standing inside a large warehouse. All I could think was that good things rarely happened to people taken to warehouses. The half-dozen men who'd delivered us stood back, weapons at the low-ready, as if awaiting orders. Hands bound, I shifted from foot to foot. One way or another, we were about to find out what was going on.

James looked at me intently, then canted his gaze toward the floor several times.

I squinted in confusion. What? He cut his gaze to where he was palming his antenna-wand against the inside of his forearm. The men had missed it in the pat-down, and now smoke drifted from where he'd just burned through his plastic wrist restraints.

I raised my eyebrows to ask if he was sure about this. He nodded.

Trying to look as casual as possible, I glanced around. One of the men's narrow nostrils flared open. Crap. With his preternatural senses, he was picking up the foul smoke. He began to come forward.

"Um, James..."

"Down!" he shouted.

I hit the floor as a flash of silver greased the air. The men cried out in pain, machine guns crackling with electrical energy. They dropped their weapons to the floor, smoke rising from their burnt hands. I used the opportunity to speak an invocation, breaking the restraints around my own wrists.

James whooped. "Now it gets *really* fun!"

He sent a silver bolt into the chest of the closest goon, then wheeled and took down another. I thrust my hand toward two men running in and shouted, *"Vigore!"*

The branching force sent one man into a wall with a bang and caught the other one in the legs, launching him toward me in a flailing arc. As he arrived, I shot a fist forward. Knuckles met mouth with a crack, and he landed in a sprawl.

"Nice one, Prof!" James shouted.

I shook my throbbing hand. "Thanks."

James ensnared the final two goons in an energy net. He whipped them around like a hammer thrower, then released them, sending them high into another of the warehouse's walls. The net broke into sparks, and the men plummeted fifteen feet into a stack of pallets.

"C'mon!" James shouted, waving me toward a large service door.

But the first shifters to go down had already healed enough to stagger upright, some reaching for their weapons. James and I took aim, but before either one of us invoked, a croaking voice echoed from above.

"Enough!"

I swung my hand upward and James his antenna-wand, but I couldn't make out anything in the shadows.

"Who's there?" James called.

"Emil," he answered. "Emil Blecher."

James looked at me. "I know that name."

"I should hope so," the voice said. "You arranged a meeting with me last night."

He croaked at his men. They reclaimed their weapons, but instead of taking aim at us, they hunkered off into shadows around the warehouse. Flaps sounded, and a large figure flew down from the rafters. He landed in front of us, a giant bird with ragged wings, a stooped neck, and a blood-red beak. But he was already morphing into a hunched man with a wrinkled pink scalp and sagging breasts.

Vulture shifter, I realized.

Though he was naked save for a pair of baggy underwear,

he looked at us coolly. One of his men appeared with a lavender robe and slippers. As the man helped Blecher into them, James turned to me excitedly.

"Makes sense I would've reached out to him," he whispered. "And it explains that weird 'yes' message on my voicemail—it was him agreeing to meet."

I wondered if it also explained the feather I'd found in the pimpmobile.

"He's an area dealer," he continued. "Santana moved the popular stuff, but Blecher is on the more boutique side of things—special product, you know. More complementary than competitive, so Santana left him alone."

"A healthy predator-scavenger relationship," I muttered.

"So, if anyone knows about this new dealer, it's gonna be Blecher."

"Unless he *is* the new dealer," I pointed out.

"Nah, not his style."

"How sure are you?"

He shrugged. "Eighty percent?"

"Great. So your twenty-percent margin of error probably explains why we were abducted at gunpoint."

"Dude, don't be such a pessimist."

"The reason you were brought here is simple." Blecher made final adjustments to his robe as he hobbled forward. "Mr. Wesson *stole* from me."

I turned to James. "Stealing from a major drug operator?" I hissed. "Again?"

"Let's get the whole story," he whispered back. "Before you make an ass of yourself twice in one day." He cleared his throat. "Mr. Blecher, sir, with all due respect, that doesn't sound like something I would do."

I snorted.

"And *if* I did"—he paused to glare at me—"it was because we were slipped something powerful last night. Something that made us do some really stupid things for which we have no memory."

"Well, we met at the Silver Cue and conducted a little quid pro quo," Blecher said. "You then proposed we shoot billiards. Having been an ace player in my youth, I agreed. I was up two thousand before you got *hot*, as they say. I ended the night down more than six, then went deeper by putting up the keys to my prize possession. "

Though I'd always thought of vultures—and by extension, vulture shifters—as sordid creatures, Emil Blecher spoke and moved with a certain elegance, as though he were from an older, more cultured era. Now he opened a crooked hand toward the SUVs we must have arrived in. Behind them was parked the pimpmobile.

James burst out laughing. "That thing is yours?"

"It's a beauty," I said quickly, shooting James an evil eye. "And it rides unbelievably, like a dream."

Blecher's elegance also made him seem dangerous, something James hadn't picked up on.

"It was only after you left, Mr. Wesson," Blecher continued, "that I was informed of your true nature. Not only a disreputable hustler, but a wizard who can shape forces. That would explain some of the improbable physics I observed."

"*Really?*" I whispered at James.

"Hey, you got us married to *Fatal Attraction*," he shot back.

"I have my car again," Blecher said. "And now I would like my money."

"Yes, take your car," James said. "Please. But I'm, ah..." He chuckled. "I'm not exactly sure what became of your money. Like I said, we lost our memories. We're only starting to piece together what happened between about eight last night and eight this morning." James drew out his wallet as he talked, pausing now to thumb through the bills. "Holy crap, there's a fat stack of hundreds in here."

"Yes, *my* fat stack of hundreds."

Blecher extended a hand toward the money, but James drew it back. "What do we get in exchange?"

"You do realize we're surrounded by armed men," I whispered, picking up the glint of gunmetal in the shadows.

"Wait, just hear me out," James said. "What I did to you, Mr. Blecher, was wrong. I admit it and I'm very sorry. You placed your bets believing you were engaged in a good-faith exchange: legit games for legit money. But *prior* to that, there was another exchange. *Squid bro ho,* you called it?"

I shook my head in dismay.

"Quid pro quo," Blecher corrected him.

"Well, we gave you something, and in return, you gave us info, right? The thing is, we lost our memories, so you didn't *really* give us anything, but you still kept what we gave you. All I'm proposing is an updated trade, one that involves us returning your money in exchange for you returning that information."

Although the argument was preposterous, James acted as though it were the most sensible thing in the world. Even *I* caught myself peeking at Blecher expectantly. After all, it would have been a shame to lose what could prove to be a major break in the case, all because we'd lost mental access to that info.

"I'll give you your Jeep," Blecher countered.

"My Jeep?" James looked around. "You took my Jeep?"

"You were so eager to drive off in my car that you left yours at the pool hall."

James let out an embarrassed laugh. "I doubt that, but all right. And that's it, we're square?"

"Hey, what about the info?" I whispered to him.

"The Jeep has all my weapons in the gun case," James whispered back. "Your stuff could be in there too."

Crap, he had a point.

Blecher cleared his throat. "I would consider giving you that information in exchange for something additional."

As he said this, a question occurred to me. What could he have wanted from us in the first place? Money? It wasn't like either of us were sitting on a pile of cash. A potion or enchanted item? But Blecher hadn't understood James's wizard abilities. A favor? That seemed more likely. And since he hadn't known about our magic, the favor must have had to do with our connection to law enforcement. Could also explain why we'd returned to the sheriff's department early that morning.

"I'm afraid James has been a little free with his use of the pronoun 'we,'" I said. "He may not remember last night, but I do. Enough, anyway. I remember our special trip to the sheriff's department."

As I cocked an eyebrow, I caught James's questioning look in my peripheral vision.

"So here's the *new* deal," I pressed. "Either repeat the info you gave us last night, and hope it's useful, or I'll take back the favor."

The smile that creased Blecher's weathered lips didn't reach his avian eyes. "You're bluffing."

"If I'm not, you're going to hate being wrong."

He glanced around, then returned his head to its natural hung position. "You asked if a new dealer had moved into Santana's void," he said at last. "I told you that until someone produced Santana's body, such a move would be too risky. So my answer to your question was 'almost certainly not.'"

James pumped a redemptive fist. "I *knew* Marge was wrong about that."

I was fighting the muscles in my face to keep them from betraying my surprise. My bluff had actually worked? "You haven't heard about anyone dealing supernatural drugs in Grimstone?" I pressed. "Even rumors?"

"Nothing that fits the description of what you're looking for."

"Then why are those four kids dead?" James asked.

"Are you sure a drug did that to them?"

As I considered his question, Blecher shifted his eyes back to me.

"I trust you'll keep up your end of this? I don't want to have to send my men to fetch you again. They're a moody flock, and accounts of them *only* picking apart dead bodies are greatly overstated."

"I will," I assured him, hoping to hell I could figure out what the favor had been and if we'd actually done it.

The vulture shifter nodded slowly and backed away. "And Mr. Wesson, I would very much like a rematch someday." He shed his robe and began morphing into a giant carrion bird. "*Fairly,* of course."

"Oh, sure thing, Mr. Blecher." James said. "Um, my Jeep?"

"My men will take you to it," he croaked as his mouth sharpened into a beak.

With a guttural cry, he flapped his ragged wings, kicking up a small storm of dust and feathers, and disappeared into the rafters.

10

Following another ride with sacks over our heads, Blecher's goons dumped us at a vacant lot on the outskirts of town, where the Jeep was waiting. One of the men spiked James's keychain into the dirt as they sped off. They clearly hadn't gotten over being slung around the warehouse. As I retrieved the keys, James circled his Jeep, eyeing it for damage.

"Nice bluff back there," he remarked.

"How did you know I was bluffing?"

"C'mon, Prof. You're talking to a pro."

"Well, it fooled Blecher," I said defensively.

"Sure, an old buzzard. Look, it wasn't bad. I just don't want you thinking you're at my level yet."

"Afraid of a little competition?"

"I'm afraid of you getting in over your head with someone who can't be played. But now that you mention it, yeah, I am afraid. Proving me wrong by getting us married? That's messed up, man."

The fight fell out of me. "I'll take care of it."

"Well, sounds like getting us kidnapped was my bad, so I suppose we're even." He paused to reconsider. "Were you serious about not being able to touch another woman until that marriage thing is annulled?"

"It's soul magic, so..."

"What would happen?"

"You could end up wang-less, among other things."

"I take it back, then. We're not even *close* to even."

While James went down to his hands to inspect the Jeep's undercarriage, I mentally updated our running tally of problems: Deputy Franks missing, Deputy Rollie freaking out, a favor to Blecher that involved tampering with something at the sheriff's department, polygamous soul-binding, memory loss... It was enough to give me vertigo, and that wasn't even counting the case of the four dead kids.

"How's it look?" I asked James as he stood.

"A lot better than I was expecting." He cupped his hands for the keys, and I tossed them over. "The weapons should be all right. I've got a magical seal on this bad boy."

He unlocked the rear of the Jeep, then spoke to the magic protecting his custom weapons compartment. After the day we'd been having, I expected the space to be empty. I was relieved to be wrong. As the door opened, a classic pump-action shotgun waxed into view, then a pair of lever-action rifles. Cases of ammo lined the compartment's other side. No cane or enchanted items that I could see, though.

James's smile shrank. "What happened to my Peacemakers?"

He was referring to his vintage Colt revolvers, his favorite weapons. He carried them in leather hip holsters, believing they made him look like an Old West gunslinger. I thought the extra-long barrels made him look ridiculous, but I understood his anxiety as he began digging behind the ammo.

"Let me know if you find anything of mine back there," I said.

"Like this wadded-up trench coat—*the hell?*" he cried, jerking his arm back out.

Something gray was attached to his hand. It trailed smoke as James whipped it around in a mad dance to rid himself of it. He finally got a hold of his antenna-wand, but it was the wrong end. I shouted a warning, but he'd already invoked. A bolt of silver energy struck him in the chest. He landed hard on his back, spuming dust, but the impact also succeeded in jarring the being from his hand.

I squinted. "Bolwig?"

The imp hovering above James with a scowling face was Madam Helga's first in command—clearly the "he" the other imps had been looking for earlier.

"Croft," the imp seethed, wheeling from James.

Without warning, he shot toward me. I made a shuffling move toward the Jeep, but the imp was already plowing into my gut. The blow doubled me over with a sick grunt. He jumped up and down on my back until I was flat in the dirt.

He returned to James, who was starting to push himself upright, and landed both feet against his forehead. James toppled onto his back again. The imp circled around, evading my swats, and kicked me once in each temple. By the time James had the correct hold on his antenna-wand, the imp was zipping away.

"Madam Helga will hear about this!" he promised.

James and I crawled over to the Jeep and sat in its shade to catch our breath. We nodded at the other that we were okay. Nothing more needed to be said. We'd just gotten our asses kicked by an imp. We had no clue how he'd ended up in the weapons compartment, either. Given what we'd learned so far, it was a coin flip as to which one of us was to blame.

At last, James struggled to his feet. "Should we head to my place?"

I nodded wearily. Maybe we would discover something there. But more than that, we just needed a break. "I don't want to hear any more about that movie whose name you can't remember, though."

"Deal," he said, clasping my hand and pulling me up.

11

As we pulled up in front of James's doublewide, I eyed the space between the sun and the canyon wall to the west. The day was getting away from us. I got out and draped my wrinkled trench coat over an arm. The pockets had been emptied of everything, including my mother's emo ball. Clinging to the improbable hope that I'd left my things here last night, I headed straight to the living room.

"Thank God," I breathed.

"Did you find Franks?" James called from another room.

"No, my suitcase."

I'd set it beside the pullout couch that served as my bed when I visited. I didn't rush up to it, though. Having already been surprised that day by a pit bull, a black mamba, and a belligerent imp, I extended my foot and nudged the suitcase. I then lifted it carefully, testing its weight, and set it on the couch. So far, so good. I released the zipper and skipped back. I watched for several moments, licking my dry lips. Finally, I retrieved a broom from the corner and used the handle to open the lid.

James returned. "Everything cool?"

"Yeah, just being extra careful. Mind covering me?"

His brow furrowed as he looked from me to my suitcase. "You want cover to unpack your toothbrush?"

"Better to be safe," I said, edging forward.

"Here, man." James handed me his antenna-wand and upended my luggage, dumping a pile of books, clothing, and toiletries onto the couch. He looked it over and declared, "All clear."

"Thanks," I said thinly, returning his wand. "Find anything?"

He shook his head. "Looked everywhere. All the rooms, backyard, wastebaskets—well, that big garbage bag on the floor in the kitchen. No clues or Franks to be found. I even checked the roof."

"The roof?"

"Never mind."

As I began organizing my things, he strolled to the window and peered through the blinds.

"We must've just come here to drop your luggage and let Annie out." He shook his head. "I should've picked her up from Loretta's."

"I'm sure she's all right."

"We are talking about the same freak, right?"

"Well, she's kept her snake alive all this time."

"You didn't catch the part about her opening up its stomach so she could watch the damn thing eat rats every day?"

"She won't have that issue with Annie. Your dog's a living garbage disposal that's always running."

His neutral grunt suggested he found some comfort in that.

"Speaking of food," I said, "I think it's time we refueled. It will help us focus."

"I've got a pack of bologna slices I can fry up," he offered. "With bread and ketchup, it's not half bad."

With half of James's kitchen stock past expiration, I doubted that very much, but I was too hungry to argue. "Sure, that'll work. Let me just—" I jerked my hand from the shirt I was planning to change into.

James rushed up, antenna-wand in firing position. "What is it?"

I dug my hand under the shirt and pulled out a glass orb the size of a tennis ball. As I turned it over, the mist inside the orb shifted and glowed, sending soothing currents up my arm and into my heart. "I thought it was in my coat, but I packed it," I said gratefully. "It's my mother's emo ball."

"Finally," James breathed, lowering his wand. "Something that isn't trying to kill us."

I chased our late lunch with a pair of antacid tablets, crunching them like candy as I opened my notepad to a blank page.

"All right." I made a vertical line down the page's center and drew a bullet point at the very top—the start of last night's timeline. "We sat down to the case file at eight p.m., which is where our memories ended. I'm guessing we reviewed the file until at least nine. That leaves about three hours before our midnight trip to the hospital. Any ideas?"

James had finished his stack of fried-bologna sandwiches and was tipped back in his chair nursing an iced tea, no hint of gastronomical distress. Like me, he'd washed his battered face and changed his shirt.

"I'm thinking we revisited the farmhouse where they found the vics," he replied.

I nodded and noted that under the 9:00 bullet point. "Sounds right. Then what?"

"Well, I've worked with Marge on a few cases that didn't involve you coming out to babysit, and she's big on door-knocking. Friends and family of the vics, potential witnesses, that sort of thing. Probably half the file right there. I wouldn't be surprised if we followed up on at least a couple of witnesses."

"And I wouldn't be surprised if we struck out," I said, flipping through the blank pages of my pad. "That's probably why we went to the hospital—to see if Dr. Bachmann could shed more light on what he'd found in their systems."

I wasn't sure if it was the calming influence of my mother's emo ball, the drug leaving our systems, or that we'd gotten a small break from the day's madness, but I could actually think straight now.

"But Bong Man decided to be a conceited ass and go all PhD," James picked up.

"No doubt. It's after midnight by this point, and we're at a dead end. But it sounds like we have a plan."

James nodded. "With a deal to eat right after."

"And the eating doesn't happen until two a.m. when we arrived at Pauline's Diner. From the way the cook described us—hooting and hollering—we were jacked up on something. We left with Loretta, came back here for Annie, and then went to Chasers... where I apparently got us married in a handicapped stall." I raised a hand in apology. "We then met Blecher at Silver Cue, explaining your cube of chalk. You and the vulture shifter played pool, and then we took off in his pimpmobile."

James shook his head in shame. "I was *definitely* jacked up on something."

"We probably headed back to the sheriff's department to do whatever favor we'd promised Blecher, then partied until Loretta left around five. Sometime after that, Franks went missing."

"We also got our faces kicked in," James reminded me.

I touched the gash beside my left eye in thought. "I'm starting to wonder if the perp showed up at the sheriff's department. That burn in your hair looks like it was magic-inflicted, and there were marks all over the breakroom walls. What if we tried to put the perp in the cell, but got thrown in ourselves?"

James nodded. "Rolls did seem a little surprised to see us."

I rendered the final bullet point at the bottom of the timeline. "Either way, we woke up in the cell at around eight this morning."

James brought the front legs of his chair down and peered over my timeline. "Looks good to me, Prof. But where does Bolwig come in?"

"Sometime before the vulture shifter, but he's not important right now. These are the two areas we need to focus on. What we did here, when we were drugged." I circled the gap between midnight and two a.m. "And what happened in here, when we lost Deputy Franks." I circled the gap between five and eight that morning.

"What was that thing you wrote down again?" James asked.

I flipped to the last page in the notepad and read it aloud:

"Swan Song." I repeated the strange phrase to myself, shaping the syllables more deliberately to see if I'd stored any power in them, but I felt nothing.

James tried it a couple times himself before shaking his head. "You must've written that a-bo," he said.

"A-bo?"

"A.B.O. After blackout. Do you still think the perp drugged us?"

"Let's find out." I consulted my watch. "Dr. Bachmann should have our results by now." Before James could suggest I be the one to talk to him, I slid him the toxicologist's business card. He made a face as he punched the number into his shattered phone, then found a speaker button on the retractable pad.

"Yeah?" Dr. Bachmann answered.

"Bong Man!" James said with false cheer. "It's your boy James, and I'm here with the professor. What's the verdict?"

"The packaging your partner brought in was clean. But the two of you—oh, boy."

"You found something?"

"A whole lot of something, and you're both full of it."

James shot me a nervous glance. "Full of what?"

"Shit." Dr. Bachmann broke into a gut-busting bout of laughter. *"Any more and the two of you could fertilize a field."*

"So we're good?" James asked uncertainly.

"Far from it. That's what I'm trying to tell you." The doctor took a moment to gather himself. *"You tested positive for tacote, and no one slips a person tacote. Your story is complete bullshit. You did that to yourselves!"*

"Come again?"

"If the quantity didn't tip you off, the hellacious taste sure as hell would've."

Before I could consider what the doctor was saying, something pricked my ankle. I plucked a stray sandspur from the folds of my sock and tossed it toward the garbage bag on the kitchen floor. James tracked it with his eyes.

"Thanks, Bong Man. Gotta run."

"What are you doing?" I asked.

"You heard him, he was being a dick."

"Not ending the call. What are you doing with that?"

James had gone over to the garbage bag and picked up the sandspur. He rolled it gingerly between finger and thumb and nodded.

"I think I know where we went after midnight."

12

"First, are you familiar with tacote?" James asked me.

"Yeah, it's a psychedelic harvested from a rare cactus of the same name. Believing it contains a god essence, some indigenous groups use it in religious rites. Produces powerful hallucinations." I'd done some additional reading on Southwest lore on the flight over, so the info was fresh in my mind.

"Not bad, Prof. And in Grimstone County, tacote *only* grows on Ute land."

"Ahh, you think we went onto their reservation?"

"No."

"Then I'm not following."

"The tribe doesn't give tacote to outsiders—it's too sacred. In fact, they don't allow outsiders anywhere *near* it, and they've got some powerful mojo on their land to make sure. I told you about their medicine man, right? Ran into him at the farmer's market some months back? Dude took one look at me, and my magic died. His way of saying, 'Leave our people alone, wizard, and we'll return the favor.' Probably the scaredest I've been since coming out here. No *way* would I go traipsing onto their turf."

"So how did tacote end up in our systems?"

He held up the spur. "We went to Celestial Gardens."

"Sounds like a theme park."

"Well, it's the wildest hippie commune in Grimstone County, so you're not too far off. I'm out there putting down nether beings every other week, it seems, and I always come back sporting a couple of these." He held up the spur. "The only place around here I've picked up this kind. See the dark little spikes on the tips?"

I nodded, impressed by his observational skills. "But if they don't give tacote to outsiders, how does Celestial Gardens have it?"

"Because Fantasia runs the show, and she's wilder than a fifth ace. She can get her hands on just about anything she deems mystical."

"And you think she slipped us this?"

He shook his head. "The doc may have been wrong about us being full of shit, 'cause we honestly don't remember, but I think he's got us on the 'doing this to ourselves' part. Think about it—we hit a dead end with the case, and Doc Bachmann was as helpful as nipples on a breastplate. Maybe we went after some hallucinogenic guidance."

I considered his theory. I'd used various enhancers in my own cases, including an Elixir of Seeing rather recently. I may even have been the one to suggest tacote—it *had* been fresh in my mind. "If we were desperate enough..." I allowed. "I've never heard of tacote causing complete memory loss, though."

"Well, Fantasia adds her own touch to these ceremonies. She could've gone a little overboard with something."

"And I'm sure you warned me in advance," I said dryly.

"Wish I could remember." He smirked as he tossed the spur into the garbage bag.

"Regardless, good detective work," I said. "Let's go talk to Fantasia and fill in the rest of that midnight-to-two gap. If we were after guidance, it might also explain what I jotted down in my pad."

I stood, but James tapped his wrist. "We need to make another call."

Crap, he was right. Marge would be finishing up her work in federal court soon, and if we didn't assure her everything was a-okay, her next stop would be Grimstone proper. I nodded. "Go ahead."

"No way. I'll dial, but you're talking."

"I thought you said I wasn't a convincing bluffer."

"You're not, but she trusts me about as far as she can throw Madam Helga, and that broad weighs half a ton. We'll work out a story beforehand—about Franks, the case, why we haven't called—and you'll deliver it."

"What if she goes off script?"

"I'll write down what to say."

"I don't think that works in real life."

"I'm a fast writer."

I shook my head in dismay. "I never thought 'mentoring' you would look like this."

"We're way past that, Prof."

We spent several minutes scripting our story, then James punched in her number and put the phone on speaker. I relaxed when the call went to the sheriff's voicemail, but James didn't end the call.

"What are you doing," I whispered.

"This is better than talking to her, believe me."

"But our strategy was a flow chart, not bulk delivery. What if she's heard from Rollie by now? Or Franks?"

James shrugged. "We're screwed either way."

"Yeah, well, you're not the one lying into her voicemail."

When the beep sounded he gestured urgently for me to speak.

I swallowed dryly. "Hi, Sheriff. It's, ah, Everson. I'm not sure if our last message got through before we lost the signal, but I wanted to give you an update. We headed out last night to follow a lead. It ended up being a poor-coverage area, partly due to some wild patterns of ley energy. A communications nightmare, basically. Heh. Anyway, James and Deputy Franks are still out there while I'm here in town grabbing some things. You know... magic things and, uh, what not." I winced. My delivery was starting to wobble. "No major updates yet, other than that this might not be a drug case. We'll explain more when we talk. Hope everything's going well over there in, ah, federal court. We're all looking forward to seeing you tomorrow. Have a nice day. Oh, and please drive—"

James ended the call.

"—safely," I finished. "Sorry. Got nervous."

"Why did you say this might not be a drug case? We never talked about that."

"I had to make it sound like we'd accomplished *something*," I said defensively. "Anyway, I was going off what Blecher told us."

James considered his phone and sighed. "Well, hopefully that'll keep her in Colorado Springs for the night."

"I think it's time we reached out to Rollie, too," I said.

"Didn't you say something about not tipping him off to our fugitive status?"

"To quote a certain wizard, 'we're way past that.' Our story only holds up if we can get him to go along."

At that moment, James's cracked phone lit up and whistled out its broken ringtone. I could feel his apprehension curdling in my own gut as we stared at one another. Odds were good it was Marge calling back.

"Don't answer," I said.

But James was looking past me now. Above the huffing of his air conditioning, I heard it too: the climbing roar of a diesel engine. Before long, the sound was drowning out the phone. James went to the window as the trailer began to shudder. Beyond the cracked blinds, a big ball of dust was barreling toward us—the product of a semi truck speeding down James's drive.

And it wasn't slowing.

13

"Crap!" James barked.

He spun, I shot to my feet, and we collided into one another. Even with our feet entangled, we somehow made it to the back door. James got it open as the semi plowed into the mobile home.

The magical ward protecting the doublewide bowed in and blew out again, launching me from the back porch. I came to a bouncing, bruising stop on my side in the dirt yard. James grunted to his own rude touchdown somewhere behind me. Meanwhile, the semi was keening off the ward. With a crunch, it snagged on a corner of the trailer and the far end began ripping away.

"No," James said as the semi's grille appeared through the wreckage of his bedroom. A pair of amps and an electric guitar spilled from the hood and were quickly crushed under the vehicle's front tires.

"*Hell* no," he said.

The pressure around us collapsed as he gathered energy and channeled it into the hand he'd planted against the ground. I remembered his buried claymores an instant before explosions began pluming from the earth. The magically enhanced force and fire lifted the front of the semi, shredding vital mechanics, and dropped it hard. As the vehicle jounced to a fiery stop, James limp-ran toward the offending driver.

Above the roaring commotion, I picked up something he couldn't: another approaching engine. I shouted a warning, but he didn't hear me.

I hobbled around to the front of the house to the sight of a second semi coming in hot. The first collision had weakened the ward. This one would take it down, along with anything in its path. I began channeling power into the protective ward, but it was too crippled and there wasn't enough time.

Dammit.

I slammed my palm against the ground, tapping into the energy matrix James had designed around his property. The driver saw me and adjusted course, aiming his semi's glinting grille at my stooped figure. Through the rippling heatwaves, I made out a beefy face with shades and a foam hat.

An actual trucker? Geez, who *hadn't* we pissed off last night?

I desperately searched the matrix as the approaching semi ate up dirt, its grille growing larger through the dust. I was almost to the point where I would have to commit or ditch when I found the energy line to the front-facing claymores. Gathering a headful of ley energy, I released it into the line with a shouted Word. The ground in front of the semi shot up into a wall of earth and flames.

When the semi reappeared, it was on its side, shoving dirt toward me in a growing mound. I backpedaled until it stopped, just a few yards away. Beyond the crushed windshield, the driver pawed at his bloodied face. Save for the hiss and crackling of fire, the rest of the canyon was quiet. No more incoming semis.

James rounded his partly demolished home, his antenna-wand in one hand, the scruff of a trucker's flannel shirt in the other. He dragged the skinny driver and dropped him to the ground beside me.

"Too dazed to talk," James said.

"Same's probably true of my guy." I nodded at the wreckage in front of me.

With several twists of his wand, James extracted the large trucker and deposited him beside his partner.

"Any ideas?" I asked as I patted them down.

"Grimstone is a major trucking hub. Maybe we got into some beef with them at Pauline's or the pool hall. Could've been anything, really."

Nodding in uneasy agreement, I took a pistol off each of them and an ankle knife from the smaller trucker. James dug out their wallets. "Jeff from Butte, Montana," he read from the larger one's license. "And... Oscar from Las Cruces, New Mexico." He pocketed the wallets. "They're not getting anything back until my damned trailer is fixed and all damages paid for. I just bought that guitar, too."

"At least your Jeep was spared."

As we looked over the smoke-blown scene, I brought my collar over my nose to filter out the diesel fumes.

James shook his head. "Who the hell sends trucks at us?"

"Someone who knew about your defenses. The first semi was meant to compromise your ward, and this one here to bring it down, along with—"

"Did you say 'dances'?" a rasping voice asked.

We looked down to find Oscar, the smaller trucker,

squinting up at us. Blood coursed from a head wound, down the gaunt lines of his face, and into his beard, where it was already drying in the late-day heat.

"No, 'defenses,'" I said carefully. "Who sent you?"

"Oh, I thought you said 'dances,'" he mumbled, ignoring my question. "I DJ on the side. Birthdays and house parties, mostly." He looked over at James's ruined trailer. "I'm also good with a hammer."

"Well, you better be good with paying for that," James told him.

He squinted from the trailer back to James in bafflement. "That was me?"

Before James could react, I took his arm and walked him several paces away. "Both their bells got rung, but I'm also picking up signs of enthrallment in their auras. They're not going to remember anything."

"Then who's responsible for the damage?"

"My *boss*," came a cantankerous voice.

We wheeled to find Bolwig hovering in a cloud of sulfurous smoke. I raised my hand and James his antenna-wand, but the imp beat us to the draw, thrusting a glazed yellow eyeball toward our faces. A psychic force struck me in the center of the brow. Swooning, I thudded to the ground beside James.

14

James was still beside me when I opened my eyes, but we were no longer on the ground in front of his trailer. We were standing in a sumptuous suite I recognized from my last visit—Madam Helga's penthouse. Only the windows were larger, the drapes lusher, the portraits grander, everything gilded to the nines.

"Da-yam," James breathed. "Talk about pimping your pad."

I looked for the witch amid the fine furniture that stretched across what seemed acres of priceless rugs. Dangling chandeliers glimmered with gold for almost as far as I could see. The impossible dimensions told me we weren't *actually* in her penthouse. She was in our heads.

"This is an enchantment," I whispered to James. "She must have cast on us through her Eye of Baba."

"It's still impressive."

But for the smell, I would have agreed. A floral perfume misted through the space, but it couldn't cover up the swampy stink that accompanied the matron witch. And with the smell came a growing dread.

"Come closer," a voice called.

I started at the familiar Russian accent. On a dais beneath the far window, a mound was taking shape across a divan. It soon resolved into the prodigious dimensions of Madam Helga. Beneath a massive updo of midnight hair festooned with enough feathers to fill an exotic bird exhibit, the witch's eyes stared from her powder-covered face.

Before I could approach her, I remembered myself. The last time, she'd demanded we remove our shoes. When I began to stoop, though, I saw we were already barefoot. We were wearing what appeared to be soiled peasant garb. Helga's imperial, pearl-studded gown, on the other hand, looked more expensive than my apartment in New York.

James mouthed a *what the hell?*

I pointed at my lips to indicate I would do the talking. There were protocols for addressing a powerful matron witch, and James was proficient in none of them. The key was to grovel—early, often, and then more often. Bowing my head toward my clasped hands, I nodded for him to follow suit.

"For real?" he whispered.

"Do you want to live?" I hissed, taking small, shuffling steps forward.

Not only had we blown away a number of her imp servants, we'd imprisoned her number one. And I had a sinking feeling Bolwig's presence last night involved the favor James owed the witch.

I cleared my throat. "Most powerful Madam Helga, we are humbled and honored to find ourselves once again in your immense presence. In the place of gifts, we hope our overwhelming awe will suffice."

I awaited her response. Instead, a horrible silence filled the enchanted space. I peeked, unable to help myself. Her gray eyes had shifted from me to James. Though his head was hung, he was sauntering forward in a way that looked almost cool. When he caught me glaring, he sighed and fell into a slovenly limp.

Better? he mouthed.

Arriving at the bottom of the dais, I adjusted my stained breeches and knelt. To James's credit, he did the same. From above her multiple chins, Madam Helga stared down at us with cold disdain.

"You puny, green driblets of toad vomit," she seethed, sitting up.

When James shifted beside me, I patted my hand toward the floor for him to stay silent.

"You lowly, pathetic flecks of worm feces." When she gathered in her breath, it seemed to suck all the air from the room. "How *dare* you challenge me!" she boomed, causing the chandeliers to rattle.

"If we could just explain—" James started.

He'd come to the same conclusion as me regarding Bolwig's errand, apparently, but I elbowed him in the side, reducing what followed to a breathless grunt. Under the thrall of the Eye of Baba, we were defenseless. Helga could do whatever she wanted to us. The only way out was going to be through, and we stood better odds if we didn't piss her off even more. That meant keeping James quiet.

"I've spent this day considering your punishment," she continued. "I settled on turning you into pair of *yaichki*. Testicles. I could not decide between fat pig or fat goat. I decided you are not worth effort."

Thank God, I breathed.

"I will just kill you."

James straightened. "Now, hold on a—"

Helga's eyes glowed red, and my partner's scream filled the penthouse. He collapsed into a writhing fit. I lunged toward Helga, images of Leia choking out Jabba the Hutt in mind. But in the next moment, I was seizing my head in both hands and releasing a scream to rival James's. A sensation like a molten-hot blade had knifed into my brain. Though psychic, it was worse than blinding. It rivaled anything I'd ever experienced, including the dread spell Helga had cast on us the last time.

That was because this wasn't a dread spell. It was a death spell.

I dug into a pocket for my mother's emo ball, but while it may have been on my actual person, it wasn't wherever *here* was. The impossible pain turned me into a desperate animal. I clawed everything I could into my mental defenses, but the blade twisted, shattering them. I kicked and went into full-body distortions, reduced now to a tortured worm trying to escape the inescapable.

With its next twist, the blade rang against something solid. Another scream pealed out, but not mine or James's.

It belonged to Helga.

The molten-hot blade evaporated. The pain withdrew. James and I stopped writhing. Up on the dais, Helga had collapsed onto her divan. Smoke drifted from her hands, which she'd crammed into the great folds of her lap. I checked my mind. My defenses were in ruins, but a band of strong, shimmering magic stood out.

"Holy crap," I muttered. "She just got thrown out by the polygamy bond."

The bond must have mistaken Helga's violent intrusion for an attempt at consummation.

"Yeah, great," James said, rubbing his head. "Now how do we throw *ourselves* outta *here*?"

I glanced around, but there was no point in running. Helga might have been wounded, but we remained under her thrall. She lay on the divan like a volcanic mound, her smoking body heaving in great gasps. Every so often, she let out a mewling cry. Once, she farted. At last, she summoned her servants.

A small platoon of imps zipped into the room and looked from her to us. I recognized several from the brawl at the hospital that morning. I was certain she was going to order them to finish us off.

"Fan me," she commanded. "Feed me."

The imps scattered and returned holding great frond-like fans and bearing platters of spoiled food. As the smoke dispersed around her hands, Helga uttered what I recognized as a healing spell. She tugged the folds of her gown from her lap, where the polygamy bond had struck, and picked over the platters. She waved most away. At last she settled on one heaped with pomegranates that had begun to blacken and cave in. Her iron teeth ripped one in half, sending rotten juice and flesh raining over us.

"That's nice," James muttered.

She glanced down. "You are still here," she said, clearly irritated by the fact we hadn't died. Either too spent or hungry to try again, she took another bite of pomegranate, sending more rotten debris over us.

"We had agreement," she said from her smacking lips. "I allowed you to talk to my girls, and you were to complete a task at time of my choosing. I sent Bolwig, and you threw him in trunk." She paused as an imp whispered something in her ear. "You called him your 'little bitch.'"

"Please forgive my partner," I said. "He is careless with his words, even in the best of times. I believe you call him a *durak* in Russian: fool. And last night, he was under the influence of a powerful drug, making him an uber *durak*. He did not intend insult. Please accept my earnest apology on his behalf."

The imp whispered to her again.

"That was *you*," Helga said to me.

James snickered and shook his head. "Man, you're such a *durak*."

"We were *both* under the influence of a powerful drug," I amended.

But Helga had returned to eating. "You made it so I could not find him," she said, no doubt an effect of the magical seal on James's weapons compartment. She waved the platter away and shook her dripping fingers over us. "I tire of talking," she declared. "I will give you one chance to fulfill bargain."

"Oh, thank you," I said sincerely. "Your largess is indeed… immense."

I nudged James, who was trying to blink a piece of pulp from his eye. "Yeah, super," he muttered.

"There is something I want," she said. "It is in Old Federal Bank, downtown. Security deposit box number ninety-two. You will bring box to me, but you are not to look inside. I forbid it, and I will know."

A bank heist? And tonight of all freaking nights?

I stammered, "H-how much time do you permit us?"

"As long as you want."

Her response was as much a surprise as a massive relief.

We could go back to finding Franks and tackling the case—as well as the trouble we'd gotten into—ideally before Sheriff Jackson returned to town. Helga wasn't finished, however.

"But you should know I have your friend."

A charge went off in my chest. *"Franks?"* I blurted out, forgetting all decorum. "You have Deputy Franks?"

An imp was whispering in her ear.

"He was the one with you when you took Bolwig," she said. "Now he is in Pleasure Palace." She produced an ornate hand mirror and breathed on the glass before turning it around. As the fog cleared, the mirror showed an image of a closed door, magic glimmering around its frame. "He is in private room. I have enspelled air inside to disappear little by little. By morning, air will be gone and your friend will be dead."

"If you would permit it," I said, "we humbly request more time. Another day perhaps, only so we may—"

"No," she thundered, cutting me off.

"Then we will embark immediately, oh matronly one." I bowed low.

"Fail me, and his will not be the *only* death," she said ominously.

"We will not fail you," I promised and looked at James.

He sighed. "Yeah, what he said. Your Vastness."

"There is one more thing."

Helga spoke to the imps. They disappeared and returned with what looked like a pair of large kettles. I recognized them as antique water pitchers. Four imps strained under the weight of each pitcher as they carried them in a staggering flight toward me and James, the spouts aimed at our mouths.

"Drink," Helga ordered.

James skewed his head from side to side. "What is this stuff? It stinks."

Fortunately, saying that something stunk was more often than not a compliment in witch-speak.

"It is to ensure you cannot hide from Eye of Baba again," Helga replied coldly. "Now drink!"

More imps flew in to brace our heads and others to wrench our mouths open. Bile-green fumes leaked from the spout that hovered over my clenched face. The instant the smell hit me, I tried to push myself away. Saying it stunk was like saying my cat, Tabitha, was difficult. It went way beyond words.

Do it for Franks, I urged myself. *Hell, do it for you and James.*

By great effort, I relaxed my jaw. The potion coated my tongue like a disease, and I began to gag and choke. The giggling imps poured faster, filling my mouth until the horrid potion spilled down the sides of my face.

15

I came to, sputtering dirt and pebbles. I was facedown in James's front yard with a cool, nighttime breeze blowing over me. My stomach garbled as I sat up, threatening to expel its contents, but both sound and sensation passed. I smacked my mouth, picking up the faintest aftertaste of the potion. That faded too, thank God.

The two truckers from earlier were gone, along with the toppled semi. Only piles of burnt dirt remained. I imagined the semi out back had been removed as well. I hurriedly checked my pockets, relieved to find my recovered wallet and my mother's emo ball.

Picking the remaining debris from my tongue, I craned my neck around. James's trailer was still in partial ruins, as if in reminder of Helga's final warning: *Fail me, and his will not be the* only *death.*

James began to stir on the ground beside me.

"Rise and shine," I said. "We've got a side adventure."

He licked his lips as he pawed the ground for his displaced cowboy hat. "The hell was that stuff?"

"Some sort of cleansing potion. Seems to have burned off the last of the tacote." My thoughts felt sharper, anyway—an unexpected boon of the encounter. "The drug must have been frustrating her efforts to scry on us."

"I don't know about any of that," James muttered as he secured his hat over his head. "Sure didn't *taste* 'cleansing.'" As I helped him to his feet, he turned to look at his trailer. "Well, crap."

"Could have been worse. A lot worse."

"No thanks to you." He smirked. "Calling her ace imp a 'little bitch'?"

"I was obviously out of my head. No thanks to *you* not warning me about your hippie friend and her creative concoctions."

"Well, were you out of your head when you called Helga a 'large ass' just now?"

"What?"

"You said her 'large ass was immense.'"

I shook my head in exasperation. "No, not 'large ass.' 'Larg*ess*.' That means generosity or—You know what? Never mind. The important thing is we know where Franks is and how to recover him."

"Think she's bluffing?"

"Helga?" I gave a dry laugh. "You really want to test her after what we just went through?"

"I just don't want to be running around for nothing. Helga's hella scary, I won't lie. But I think I'm more afraid of Marge."

"When Bolwig didn't return last night, Helga must have sent out some trucking muscle," I said, working it out as I spoke. "When they didn't find him or us, they could've gotten lucky and spotted Franks on his way home. They took him to

Helga and stashed his cruiser in a warehouse. With his memory shot, she couldn't interrogate him, so she locked him in the Pleasure Palace as collateral."

"I can think of worse places to be imprisoned," James remarked. "Even with my air running out."

"I'm sure you can. Anyway, on the slim chance she is bluffing, it's not like we can go to the hotel to check. The place is swarming with imps. They catch us sneaking around, and Helga *will* turn us into an animal's swinging appendage or find a way to kill us dead. She's definitely not bluffing there."

"Yeah, that broad has some issues. But a bank job?"

"Hey, it's the bargain we made—correction, *you* made with her—the last time. The one you claimed was your problem, not mine? Not only is the bargain binding, Franks's life depends on it now."

"Binding, like our marriage to Loretta?"

"In case you didn't notice, that saved our butts back there."

His smirk became a laugh. "Like you knew that last night."

"Maybe not, but my magic did."

I considered the symbiosis between magic and mages—what my Order called a "luck quotient," stronger in some mages than others. *Very* strong in me, apparently.

"Man, why do you keep flexing your magic?" James said. "You insecure or something?"

Heat broke over my face, suggesting he'd hit a nerve. When we first met, I'd been bothered that James had received more training than me and was more proficient with his invocations, but I let it go. That was until the Order decided I was the more senior wizard and sent me to mentor him. I may have solved more cases and overcome bigger threats than him, but how much of that was talent and how much my luck quotient? And if the second, what were my qualifications to be mentoring anyone?

Maybe I *was* flexing as a way to compensate for my doubts.

"If that's how I've come off, I'm sorry," I said. "But look, the clock's ticking, and we've got some prepping to do if we're going to pull this off."

"Good thing two-thirds of Grimstone's law enforcement is either out of town or a hostage," he remarked.

As absurd as it sounded, he was absolutely right. That was the last twenty-four hours in a nutshell: a heaping pile of absurdity. What began as a chuckle of acknowledgment turned into a fit of chortling and then cackling.

"You all right, man?" James asked, looking concerned.

"Has anyone… in the history of wizarding," I gasped, "ever been… this fucked?"

The hysteria seeped into my gut and lungs, and I doubled over, unable to stop. The laughter caught James up until we sounded fit for an asylum, wheezing and screaming into the desert night. When coyotes answered in the distance, we laughed even harder. Just when I thought I might pass out, the hysteria relented.

"Oh, God," I breathed, wiping away tears. "I needed that."

"C'mon." James slung his arm around me. "I'll brew us some coffee. Assuming I've still got power." As we ascended the steps to his severely canted mobile home, we fell into another fit of laughter.

James did have power, miraculously, and after we'd gotten control of ourselves, he brewed a halfway decent pot of coffee. I had to prop up two of the legs on his kitchen table to compensate for the home's new lean. We laid out all of our available magical implements, arcane books, and spell ingredients across the table, and it became command central.

I pulled out my notepad. "All right, what can you tell me about the bank?"

James began pacing the uneven kitchen, flipping and catching a quarter while keeping his balance. "Gorgeous old building on Main. The Brunholds built it, and dwarves know their stone, so the structure itself is solid. The main door and security systems look pretty standard, though. Bolt locks, contact alarms, CCTV cameras."

"Should I be worried that you've already cased this place?" I asked.

"Nah, just one of those 'what if?' games I've played while waiting for a teller. And don't tell me you don't play it too."

"I don't, actually, but this is good. We can handle locks, alarms, and cameras with basic spells and invocations."

"Yeah, but the safety deposit boxes are inside the vault, and just wait'll you see the thing." He blew out his breath. "The door is one of those big round ones with the shiny wheels. The bank displays it proudly, and I can't blame 'em. It's got that work-of-art thing going, but it's also a solid ton of metal outfitted with a serious locking mechanism. The whole thing's set inside walls of reinforced stone. That eliminates brute force."

"With the right leverage, might we crack the bolts with a spell?"

James shook his head before I'd even finished. "No space

between the vault door and frame. We're talking seamless. You couldn't even slide that sheet of paper in there."

"Fire?" I suggested. "Dragon sand might melt out the metal."

"Same problem. And even if we *could* squeeze in some fire, the vault door uses a copper alloy to break up heat."

"You really have played the 'what if?' game on this."

"Yeah, it can get slow in this town." He caught the quarter he'd been flipping and began swimming it between his fingers.

"What about the lock itself? Does it take a key?"

"Key and code."

"Who has those?"

"The owner and bank managers, I reckon."

If it were just a key, we probably could have found one in one of the bank's offices. For the code, we'd need to involve a person.

I bit the end of my pencil in thought. My wizard's voice only tended to work on beings of lower intelligence, so compelling a person was never a sure thing. That left force and deception. I didn't have the thumb-breaking mentality for the first, but the second was a possibility. I was looking to see if we had the ingredients for illusory magic when James spoke.

"There's another option."

I looked over. "What's that?"

"Translocation."

"Yeah, which neither of us can—" I stopped and stared at him. "Are you telling me you can *translocate*?"

When he returned a guarded nod, I felt the strange competitiveness boiling up again. Translocation was an advanced spell, one that I was still years—if not decades—

from being able to master. I began tapping my right foot irritably, but remembering my insight outside, I made it stop.

"Sorry." I cleared my throat. "Go on."

"Elsie could do it," he explained, referring to his first mentor. "I used to beg her to show me. She always said I was too young and inexperienced, all that, but she got drunk one night and walked me through it."

"And it worked?"

"Over a really short distance. Inches. She just wanted to shut me up, and I'm pretty sure it was mostly her doing the translocating. But I practiced in secret for a while after. Took me a year to do it myself. I got up to a few feet before I stopped."

"Why would you give up something like that?" I asked in disbelief.

"I never liked the feeling. It's freaky, man. Like maggots crawling all through you." He pocketed his quarter with a shudder. "And I never really needed to use it. Not for those kinds of distances. I'd rather jigger a lock to get inside somewhere than translocate. But in this case, we don't have a choice."

"Are you sure you can clear the door?"

There were tales of magic-users translocating into walls and having to undergo gruesome amputations to free themselves. If James hadn't volunteered himself, I would never have asked him to take that risk.

"Shoot, with room to spare. It can't be more than three feet."

Though he said it confidently, I sensed an undercurrent of bravado.

"Maybe you should practice," I suggested. "Make sure you've still got it in you."

"Nah, it's not the kind of thing you lose—it just takes a lot of power. And if I'm gonna go for two tonight, I'm better off saving my amps."

"What about pulling the safety deposit box?"

"I've got something for that, too."

He disappeared to rummage inside a closet. I wondered, not for the first time, what Helga was having us steal and whether it was going to amount to grand larceny or just petty theft. Though I supposed breaking into a bank was felony enough. When James returned, I expected him to show me a magical lock-picking implement, but he was wielding a standard drill. He fired it a few times for effect.

"Diamond bit," he said. "It'll bore right through the lock. I just need to charge the batteries."

I nodded and looked over the notes I'd made, each block representing a step in the operation. Assuming James *could* translocate in and out of the vault, we had the heist covered. It was ballsy, not to mention highly criminal, but right now Franks's life took precedent. With a sigh, I closed the notepad.

"All right, I'll get started on the potions."

16

Weeds whacked the Jeep's undercarriage as James pulled into a vacant lot two blocks from Main Street and parked behind a collapsing shed. I handed James one of the two beer bottles I'd been cradling—the best receptacles I could find for the stealth potion I'd cooked on his stove. He held his up.

"To a successful job," he proposed.

We clinked necks and downed the stealth potions. The tingling began in my gut, and it wasn't long before we appeared specter-like to the other. To anyone else, including CCTV cameras, we were effectively invisible.

From my footwell, I lifted a leather saddlebag that James had bought locally and converted into a satchel. Digging past various tools for the night's job, I pulled out two pairs of latex gloves, and James and I snapped them on. We bumped fists and hustled down a narrow side street until we reached Main.

It was after midnight, and Grimstone's main thoroughfare

was empty. Opposite us rose Old Federal Bank, two stories of stout, dwarf-hewn stone.

"Twenty minutes," I reminded James. That was when the potion would peak, and I wanted to be out of there well before then.

"We'll be at the Jeep in ten," he promised.

Wishing I shared his confidence, I followed him across the street. As we hunkered in front of the bank's glass doors, my heart slammed. A steely blend of nerves, excitement, and *this is freaking crazy*.

For his part, James appeared steady. Nodding that it was "go time," he inserted the tip of his antenna-wand into the keyhole and uttered an unlocking incantation. Silver light glowed, and a clunk sounded. He withdrew the wand, already pointing beyond the glass at the lobby cameras—four of them. The stealth potion may have concealed us, but it wouldn't hide the door's motion.

Nodding, I whispered, *"Oscurare."*

The shadows around the cameras billowed like storm clouds and gathered over the lenses. Pressing a charged quarter against the frame where the contact alarm was mounted, James pulled the door open. We both slipped in. Grinning, James dropped the quarter into the saddlebag's side pocket. I relaxed my invocation, releasing the shadows. For anyone reviewing the footage, those couple seconds would look like an innocuous blur.

"There she is," James whispered.

The vault was to the right of the teller counter, set back behind a decorative gate. Its floor-to-ceiling door was as impressive as James had described it, and we were soon standing before the colossal metal barrier.

"You sure you're up to this?" I whispered.

We'd already gone over the risks, but I wanted to remind him that he still had an out. He nodded—first to himself, it seemed, then to me—and aimed a finger at the vault door.

"No going back now."

"There is, actually. The way we came in. I'm just saying that if you're having second thoughts, we can try something else."

"I've schemed it out dozens of times in my head. This is the only way we're getting inside this beast." By his tone, I could tell he'd talked himself into the translocation. There would be no dissuading him.

"All right, but remember that a lot of these vaults have tables inside for folks to sit down and organize their deposit boxes, usually in the middle, so you don't want to overshoot the door by much."

His pointed finger faltered as he regarded the door anew.

"You still okay?" I asked.

"Pass me the drill."

I produced the tool from the saddlebag and handed it to him. Facing the vault door, he set his booted feet apart and held his arms akimbo. He took several deep breaths, in through his nose and out through pursed lips until he sounded like a bellows. On the sixth breath he held the inhalation. My ears registered a shift in pressure.

Then, in a glimmer of silver, James was gone.

I stared at the spot for two full seconds, stunned. A part of me had doubted he could actually translocate, but it quickly shifted to worry over whether he'd made it all the way through—or perhaps gone too far. I strained to listen beyond the vault door. I opened my mouth to call his name before stopping. All that time planning the heist and we hadn't thought to come up with code names?

"Partner?" I tried.

No answer. I swallowed dryly and called out again.

Seconds ticked by. Sweat clung coldly to my face.

"I'm here," came James's distant voice at last. "Just needed to knock out the camera."

I slumped in relief, the mental images of his body grafted to the door or a table dissipating. Now I pictured his gaze running along the numbers until he reached box ninety-two. A moment later, the faint whine of his drill started up.

As the diamond bit chewed into metal, my anxiety reared its head. Would this be the step that foiled us? Minutes passed as he started and stopped the drill until we were beyond his promised ten. The effect of the stealth potion would be waning soon. But when the drill stopped next, it was followed by a metallic clunk.

"Got it!" James announced. "Stand back."

I pumped a fist—take that anxiety!—and cleared the spot where he'd recently translocated from. I waited in the anticipation of getting out of there with the box and swapping it for Franks. But then James's muffled voice returned.

"Small problem."

I stepped forward. "What's up?"

"I can't seem to get any magic going in here."

"Nothing?" I asked, refusing to believe a modern bank had hired a magic-user to ward its vault.

Then it hit me. If the dwarves had constructed the vault along with the bank, they would have baked in some anti-magic as a matter of course. Anti-magic that could still be effective, even a century later. A basic reveal spell showed me a dim copper glimmer in the stonework around the vault's door. Out here, we could cast, no problem. But inside the sealed vault, James was effectively snuffed.

"Not a damned thing," he confirmed a moment later.

I swore to myself. How could I have been so stupid? I described the situation to him as well as I could through the solid door: The anti-magic worked by repelling ley energy. Barring a breach of some kind, he had none to draw from, and the innate energy in his blood wouldn't be enough to power a translocation.

"Are you saying I'm *stuck* in here?" he shouted.

"Hold on, let me think." I paced the front of the vault before tuning into my magic.

If you've got any luck for me, I thought at the mysterious tides shifting inside me, *I could sure as hell use some right now.*

Beyond the glass doors to the bank lobby, a green-on-white cruiser rolled past. Deputy Rollie? I drew back on instinct. That *wasn't* the kind of luck I'd been asking for. Or was it? A glimmer of an idea took hold.

"Wait here," I called to James.

"You're leaving me? Hey, where you going?"

But I was already hustling toward the front doors. Drawing the charged quarter from the saddlebag, I imitated what I'd seen James do. No alarms sounded, and I was soon on the sidewalk outside the bank. Rollie's cruiser had stopped at a red light a block away. I ran toward him, but the light cycled green.

"Wait!" I shouted, but he couldn't hear me.

Not knowing whether I was about to do something incredibly clever or incredibly stupid, I aimed an arm at him. Force blew from my palm, and the cruiser's rear window collapsed in a sheet of shattered glass. The brake lights lit up. Rollie sat there for a moment before his cruiser heaved into reverse.

Guess I'm about to find out...

17

Spilling pebbles of window glass, the cruiser skidded to a stop beside me. Rollie threw his door open but then crouched with his revolver and covered both sides of the street. Though the force invocation had burned through some of my stealth potion, I was still too spectral for him to make out.

"This is the Grimstone County law!" he called in a slurred voice.

When his gaze shot past me, I noted his red, watery eyes. Great, the deputy was sloshed. Attempting to get his attention suddenly felt dangerous. I crouched on the other side of the cruiser.

"Don't shoot!" I called. "It's Everson!"

Because James and I were both under the spell of the same potion, we'd been able to communicate fine. For Rollie, though, my voice would have sounded faint, barely audible above his breaths, if at all.

"You're under arrest for attacking an officer," he called

across the street. Then, seeming to realize he didn't have a suspect yet, he slurred, "Show yourself…"

I considered disarming him, but without my cane, I lacked precision, and I didn't want to hurt him. Instead, I invoked a rudimentary protection around myself, mainly to burn through the rest of the stealth potion.

"Rollie!" I tried again. "It's Everson!"

He heard me this time. "Where are you?"

"On the other side of your vehicle. I'm unarmed."

I upped my protection as he shuffled around the car. The last time we'd talked, I'd been in a holding cell with James and his dog. More than sixteen hours had passed since, and I had no idea whether he'd contacted Marge. I could only imagine what she would have told him to do if he found us—attempt to hold us until her return, for starters. He arrived around the rear fender and stared past me.

"Over here," I said, waving.

He staggered back in surprise and fumbled his weapon into firing position. I showed him my empty hands. He blinked stupidly for several seconds before deciding I was harmless. He lowered his weapon again.

"Are you dead or something?"

"No," I said, straightening. "This is just an effect of a potion."

He took in my spectral state for another moment before peering around blearily. "Someone just shot out my window."

"That was me. We need your… help," I said, not so sure anymore. "How are you doing?"

He looked at me, then up at the night sky, his body wavering over his feet. Before I could steady him, he fell back against his vehicle. "I've looked everywhere," he sobbed, "but I can't find Franks."

"Does Sheriff Jackson know?"

As tears dripped from his lampshade mustache, he shook his head. "I left her a message. Told her y'all were out of service range. But she keeps calling. I finally went to the bar. I'm no good with this kind of stress."

I pumped a mental fist. Exactly the message I'd left on Marge's voicemail—maybe Fortune was beginning to smile on us. To keep the streak going, though, we needed Rollie on board. The next moments would be crucial, but first I wanted to know something. "Franks's midnight check-in," I said. "Where did he say we were going?"

"To the communes," Rollie replied.

"Celestial Gardens?"

"Yeah, but I already drove out there, and no one's seen him since last night. What am I gonna do?" he blubbered.

I gripped his sweaty shoulder. "I know where Franks is."

He sniffled and tried to focus through his eye-glaze. "Y-you do?"

"Yes, but he only has a few hours to live. If we're going to recover him, you need to do *exactly* what I tell you." I pushed power into my wizard's voice. Rollie wasn't dumb, but he *was* inebriated. Almost as good.

He straightened from the vehicle and wiped his entire face with his sleeve.

"I'm listening," he said.

"I'm still telling you that it's impossible," the bank manager complained as he got out of his station wagon in front of the bank. "We check the vault at the end of the day by monitor, and we also do a walk-through."

"Well, we have to answer these kinds of calls," Rollie said.

The deputy still sounded drunk, but the bank manager seemed too irritated to notice. He was an older man with glasses and a messy wreath of mustard-brown hair. He hadn't liked being woken up, and he'd liked driving into town even less, but Rollie thought he would be the easiest bank official to work with.

"Probably a kid playing a prank," the manager muttered. "I doubt a call can even be *made* from inside the vault."

"It was a weak signal," Rollie said, then hiccupped.

The manager gave him a skeptical squint before shifting his gaze to me. "Who's he?"

I was standing behind Rollie, my shoulder and hip braced against him to prevent him from losing his balance. The stealth potion had long since petered out, fortunately, so I was no longer an apparition.

"A consultant," I answered for Rollie. "The deputy is showing me the ropes."

The manager snorted. "Well, this is a highly unusual call out, I can assure you."

He punched a code into his phone to deactivate the building alarm, then unlocked the front door. I guided Rollie inside, holding the crook of his arm. As we crossed the lobby, the vault door glinted from the shadows in back. With an anguished start, I saw I hadn't closed the decorative gate. Fortunately, the manager was busy searching through his keys as he led the way toward an office.

"I'll show you the live feed so you can see for yourselves."

As he unlocked the office and flipped on lights, I took Rollie's hand and made it grip the doorframe. *"Stay,"* I whispered.

I backed away, then turned and hurried toward the gate.

We had tried calling James several times, but the manager was right about the vault blocking phone signals. The dwarves' magic didn't help. I itched to warn James now, but I wouldn't be able to raise my voice enough. I closed the gate and returned to the office, arriving just as the manager was discovering the vault camera was out.

"That's odd," he said. "It was working earlier."

"Could explain how your employees missed the guy stuck inside," I offered.

He pushed past us and led the charge to the vault. At a locked panel beside the vault door, he jabbed in a code, then produced the longest key from the bunch in his hand.

"Don't worry!" I called. "The deputy and bank manager are here! We're going to get you out!"

But it was hardly enough warning. The manager had already inserted the key, and with a turn of the wheel, the cylinders released from the frame with a metal-on-stone scrape. Ley energy began coursing inside.

"Jiminy Christmas!" the manager exclaimed as the door opened.

I parked Rollie at the gate and rushed up. I expected to find James standing stock still in the center of the vault, the incriminating safety deposit box in one hand and the even more incriminating drill in the other. Instead, he was slumped against the vault's far end, his chin resting on his chest, legs splayed.

The manager dashed around the table in the center of the vault—I'd been right about that—and knelt beside him.

"Sir?" he said, giving James a gentle shake. "Are you okay, sir?"

I was getting worried myself. Had the anti-magic hurt him? But when James stirred and peered up, I saw he was acting. "Thank God someone came," he croaked, rubbing his eyes. "Thought I was a goner for sure."

"What happened?" the manager demanded. "How did you become locked in here?"

"I was let inside to put something in my box. The door closed, and no one opened it again. I was so scared." Before the manager could start probing into specifics, James asked him, "How much air did I have left, you think?"

He chuckled nervously. "Oh, you needn't have worried. The vault is ventilated."

"Do my fingernails look blue to you?" James splayed them above his lap. "I think they look blue."

As the manager examined them, James cut his eyes to my left. In the wall of safety deposit boxes was a glaring hole between numbers ninety-one and ninety-three. James had also left his antenna-wand inside the slot. I moved over until I blocked them from view. James pushed himself up suddenly and grasped the manager's hands.

"I'm gonna pass out if I don't get some fresh air in the next five seconds."

The manager, who was no doubt fearing negative publicity, not to mention a lawsuit, was only too eager to help. "Sure, sure, come with me, sir." As they stepped out, I caught the oblong lump in the back of James's shirt and pants—the concealed deposit box and drill—but we weren't out of the woods yet.

"Deputy, could you close the vault behind us?" the manager called back.

Rollie began to comply, but I waved for him to stop. There was still the matter of the stolen box. When the bank noticed it missing, they would review the security footage and discover the box had been there right up until tonight's incident. At first I'd thought James had forgotten his wand, but now I believed he'd anticipated the problem and left the wand for me to remedy. I didn't give him enough credit sometimes.

With the anti-magic fighting the entering ley energy, I couldn't get too fancy.

A minor illusion, like the kind hiding my home library, should do the trick.

From the saddlebag, I produced a nugget of gold that James had found on his property and placed it in the slot's opening. Incanting softly, I circled the wand over the neighboring box. capturing its image. I then coaxed the image over the opening, locking it in place via the potent energy-storing properties of the gold. After blurring the last digit in the number, I stood back. Passable, but I needed a neutral observer.

"Does anything look out of place?" I asked Rollie.

He followed the aim of the wand, eyes struggling to focus. "Out of place, how?"

Good enough. Hopefully the footage would be irretrievable by the time the box's owner returned. We closed the vault door and joined James outside.

"I assure you, we will do *everything* we can to make it up to you," the manager was telling him. "We'll start by moving you to an executive account."

James had him on his back foot, but there were too many plot holes. While James might have been a bank customer, he wasn't renting a safety deposit box and so had no reason to have been in the vault in the first place. What we really needed was for the manager to forget tonight had happened. My earlier ability to influence Rollie's drunken mind gave me an idea.

I circled a hand for James to keep the manager engaged and pulled a small squeeze bottle from the saddlebag. This piece of improvised potion-storage held a sleeping concoction. Catching on, James looked up suddenly.

"Whoa, did you see that?"

"What?" the manager asked, following his gaze skyward. I reached around and squirted a thin line of potion across the top of his shirt. Just enough to send a light curtain of fumes into his face.

"I keep seeing these spots of light," James said. "Probably my PTSD acting up. I got trapped down a well when I was eight. If my dog hadn't gone for help, I'd still be at the bottom of that thing."

The manager reassured him everything was fine while offering ever more banking perks. When his words became disjointed, I tapped his shoulder. He staggered around and struggled to focus on my face.

"Go home," I said. "Go back to bed and sleep deeply. In the morning, this will all have been a dream."

With the potion softening his cognition, my wizard's voice drove straight to his suggestion centers. The manager's brow softened and he released a dreamy chuckle. "That would be nice, yes."

Seeming to have forgotten James and the vault incident, he plodded to his car and got in. He waved without really seeming to know who we were and rolled out slowly. I jerked my head at Rollie.

"Better tail him," I said. "Make sure he gets home okay."

"We'll grab Franks and meet you back at the department," James called after him.

Rollie started up his cruiser and weaved down the street, the drunk escorting the half-asleep.

When they turned a corner, I gripped my knees and exhaled out the accumulated stress from the last hour. I even got a little lightheaded. James chuckled. I looked over to find him beaming at the bank.

"Man," he said. "That was even more kickass than I imagined."

18

"Did you see how freaked out that dude was when he saw me lying there?" James laughed. "Easiest con job ever."

"Crack work," I agreed. "But how did you know we were coming in?"

The Jeep's tires skidded around a turn as we sped toward Madam Helga's. Although there was still plenty of time until first light, the sooner we made the swap for Deputy Franks, the better. I didn't trust witches.

"I figured you were either gonna try some big-time magic," James replied, "or get someone from the bank to open the vault. There was nothing I could do about option A, so I played B. And with option B, I figured your story would be that someone had gotten locked in, so I refined my role accordingly. Out of all the plausible lies, that one had the best chance of action. I'm surprised you knew that, Prof."

"I'm learning," I said with a frown. "But a lot of that credit goes to Rollie. I caught him driving past and he agreed to call the manager. The 'locked inside' story was much more plausible coming from him, even drunk."

James chuckled. "My man, Rolls. Thought I smelled some fumes on him."

"And we're in luck. He hasn't told Marge anything. He also confirmed that we went to Celestial Gardens after the hospital last night."

"Then what's with that worry chasm on your forehead? Rolls is in our corner now, right? Marge is still out of town, and in the dark. And this beauty right here is our ticket to getting Franks back." He slapped the drilled-out deposit box, which I was holding protectively on my lap. I'd checked the number so many times that it was becoming a compulsive tic. I checked it again, just to be sure.

"We still have to figure out the favor we did for Blecher," I said. "We also need to annul our marriage, ideally before I return to New York. And I'd *really* like to recover the rest of my magical items. Oh, and then there's the small matter of the supernatural killer. You know, the case I was brought here to help solve."

"It'll all work out, you'll see. Happy thoughts, Prof."

I could tell from the wild gleam in his eyes that he was still riding high from the heist. I wished it had had the same effect on me.

"If we get Franks, I'll feel slightly better," I allowed.

"We *will* get Franks. So... what do you think's inside the box?"

It would have been as easy as opening the lid to find out, but Helga had forbidden it, and I didn't dare give her an excuse to negate the deal. A jolting thought occurred to me. "You didn't peek when you were in the vault, did you?"

"Oh, c'mon, man. You think I'm the kid in those impulse-control experiments who eats the marshmallow straight up?"

"Well, did you?"

He hesitated. "I ate the marshmallow—but *only* because I was really hungry that day at school."

"I'm talking about looking inside the box."

"After what Helga did to us?" He peered at me sidelong. "All right, I won't lie. Almost, but no."

"Remind me to give you two marshmallows later."

"Real funny, Prof. For real, though, any guesses?"

I slanted the box one way, then the other. Something slid inside, thumping softly against each end. "Could be anything," I said. "Something Helga's had her eye on... something she believes is rightfully hers. Regardless, after this is over, we're going to need to figure out whose this is and how to reimburse them."

"My gold nugget wasn't enough?"

He hadn't been thrilled when I'd told him about leaving it in the box's slot to maintain the illusion.

"We'll see," I said.

"Man, I was counting on that for part of my retirement."

"Good thing you're still young, then. But let's deal with one problem at a time."

Ahead, Helga's hotel was rising above the grim trucking lots and warehouses with the pomposity of a Russian palace. Floodlights illuminated the pale-blue façade and highlighted gold-topped columns and ornate balconies.

As James pulled into the main lot, I switched to my wizard's senses. The imps zipping around the hotel stopped suddenly and amassed in an agitated cloud. Not only did they recognize us; they were sporting for a rematch.

"Imps incoming," I announced.

James frowned and stepped on the gas.

"Hey, whoa, what are you doing?"

"Hold on to something."

I pinned the box under an arm and seized the door handle as James raced his Jeep past parked rigs and launched us over a speed bump. The arriving imps thumped off the windshield in bursts of smoke. No sooner had we jounced to a landing, than we were hitting a second speed bump. My head whiplashed around.

James swerved to pick off some stragglers, then turned onto the hotel's circular drive. He squealed to a stop before the main doors.

"We're VIP," he said defiantly.

We got out, and I hurried toward the hotel, carrying the safety deposit box like a football while massaging my sore neck. But when I turned, James was still at his Jeep, drawing his pump-action shotgun from the rear compartment.

"Let's just deliver this and get Franks," I said.

"I'm sick of being disrespected by these little shits."

He backed toward me, weapon aimed at the reorganizing imps, several already streaking toward us. I pulled out the antenna-wand, which was bent now. As imps circled us, I tried to straighten it with my teeth before giving up and swapping it for my mother's emo ball. James panned the twin barrels across the imps' chattering numbers.

"Unless you want a face full of salt," he growled, "you best stay back."

"We're here at Madam Helga's request," I called, dispensing with the customary fawning. "We have something for her."

A grunting imp shouldered his way through the masses and shot toward me. When I held up the glowing ball, he stopped suddenly. It was Helga's lead imp, Bolwig. The same imp I'd insulted and locked inside James's trunk the night before. Under his stick nose, his pursed lips quivered angrily.

"Give me the box!" he snapped.

"Not until we get our friend back," I said.

Bolwig considered the emo ball, scowled some more, and disappeared. He returned an instant later, holding the same gilded hand mirror from our meeting with Helga. The witch's fleshy face stared from the glass.

"Show me," she said, meaning the box.

I held it up so she could see the number and the "Old Federal Bank" stamp in the metal. A small smile pinched her lips.

"Relinquish it to Bolwig."

I lowered the box. "Not until you release Franks."

Bolwig drew himself up. "How dare you order Madam Helga, you pathetic wizard scum!"

Like James, I didn't care anymore. We'd done what she asked, and I was tired of groveling.

Helga sighed heavily. "Show them."

Bolwig remained hovering with the mirror. "But Madam—"

"Show them!" she thundered.

Whatever was in the box, she wanted it—badly. With a scowl, Bolwig waved for James and me to follow him through the hotel's front doors. The remaining imps dispersed in disappointment. Bolwig led us through the marble lobby and bar area, where Helga's girls, bolstered by seduction enchantments, sweet-talked potential clients. James's gaze lingered on them as we left the lobby for a corridor of private rooms. I felt the magically sealed door before I saw it, the same one Helga had shown us while we were under her thrall. James picked up on the thrumming energy too.

"Seems like overkill," he said.

"No kidding, but Helga doesn't seem to do small portions."

Bolwig planted a ragged wing in the air and wheeled around to face us. "He's in there. Now give me the box."

I jerked it out of reach of his grasping hands and held up the emo ball.

"Not until you release him," I said slowly, as if repeating instructions to a child.

Helga must have heard me through the mirror because the magic around the door's frame shone brightly before glimmering out. A series of clicks and creaks followed—the wood settling—then the door released.

"Franks?" James called. "You in there, buddy?"

I expected the deputy to come stumbling out in equal parts confusion and elation. Instead, a violent force rocked the door open. The figure who appeared wasn't six feet plus and lanky, but four feet tops and built like a barrel. That's because it wasn't Franks the deputy; it was Tjalf the dwarf.

"Whoa," James said, backing away.

19

Tjalf stared back at us, his ginger beard in disarray, his chest huffing like a locomotive. Then, as if his rage-dial were being spun to ten, his bushy eyebrows crushed down over bulging, bloodshot eyes.

"You two!" he roared.

My mind was so befuddled by the curveball of his appearance that I was too slow to react to the box being yanked from my grasp. With a delighted cackle, Bolwig flew it out of my leaping reach.

"Madam Helga considers the bargain fulfilled," he said.

"Wait!" I shouted. "The deal was for Franks, and this isn't Franks!"

"No-o-o," Bolwig said slowly, mimicking my voice from earlier. "The deal was for the one with you when you kidnapped me, and that was the dwarf."

There was too much going on for me to replay my meeting with Helga word-for-word, but witches excelled at guile, and chances were good she'd never specifically told me she had the deputy.

"Then where is he?" I demanded. "Where's Franks?"

"Not our problem." Bolwig grinned. "You can show yourselves out."

As the imp wheeled clumsily with the safety deposit box, I swapped the emo ball for the antenna-wand. *"Vigore!"* I shouted.

Forgetting the wand was bent, I watched the force invocation discharge at an angle and crater the wall well shy of Bolwig, who was crowing out a victory chant as he zig-zagged down the corridor.

James pivoted from Tjalf, whom he'd been trying to assuage, but before he could blow Bolwig from the air with a rock-salt shell, the dwarf plowed into him, knocking the shotgun from his grasp and James to the floor.

"Don't let him fly away!" James called to me.

By the time I retrieved the gun, Bolwig and the box were gone and Tjalf was straddling James's back, pounding him with both fists.

"Taffy, buddy," James grunted, covering his head with his arms. "Let's talk about this."

But the dwarf was beyond reason. And with his innate strength, he could easily hospitalize James—or worse. I took a running start and drove my lowered shoulder into the dwarf's side. It was like colliding into a tree trunk. I bounced off him, head rattled, pain shooting down my arm, while Tjalf didn't so much as budge.

"You swindling, dwarf-stripping, no-good..." he seethed as he continued to pummel James.

A door to a private room banged open, and a red-faced man emerged, upset we were disturbing his session. He looked over the scene and closed the door again, wanting no part of whatever this was.

James was covering himself well, but for how much longer? I drew my antenna-wand, adjusted for the angle, and shouted, *"Forza dura!"* The invocation caught Tjalf under his beard, snapping his head back and sending him from James in a rear somersault. He landed against a wall, shaking the corridor.

I helped James to his feet. "You all right, buddy?"

"More tender than I normally prefer, but yeah," he groaned.

I pressed the shotgun into his grasp and readied my wand, but my force blast seemed to have taken the starch out of the dwarf. Though he was still fuming as he got to his feet, he was no longer the raging bull of moments earlier.

"Taffy, listen to me, buddy," James panted. "However you ended up in here, we're sorry. We have no memory of last night, and all this time we thought you were Deputy Franks. Hell, we just robbed a bank to get him out of here, but we're just as happy to have sprung you instead. Well, almost as happy, 'cause without Franks we're gonna be in deep shit with the sheriff in a few hours, but you get what I'm saying."

I backed James up with a vigorous nod, even though none of that would've made sense to anyone but us.

Tjalf's eyes glowered above his flaring nostrils. His pinstripe suit, sweat-stained and ripped along several seams, testified to his efforts to escape. That explained Helga's overkill on the locking spell—dwarves were resistant to middling magic. But I was more interested now in how he'd ended up with us last night.

"Can we take you somewhere?" I offered.

He glowered at us for another moment, then grunted and eased his hunched shoulders down. "Celestial Gardens."

"No way," James laughed. "We're going there too."

"Wait," I said, "you were with us at Celestial Gardens last night?"

"Not *with* you. I went out there to talk land business with Fantasia. I was coming, and you were going. Met in the lot. I wanted to settle up over the two of you busting into my compound and stripping me to my skivvies, but you had that deputy with you. And then you..." His voice went mild as he glanced down at his scuffed shoes. "Then you invited me out for burgers at Pauline's. Your treat."

That explained the high volume of patties the cook had had to flip last night. Most of them ended up in Tjalf. With Charlie's poor vision, and the dwarf's short stature, Charlie hadn't seen Tjalf from his service window. But had we really buried the hatchet with Tjalf over steak burgers? If so, last night may not have been all bad.

"Then you asked me along for drinks at Chasers," Tjalf continued. "Didn't realize you two were so crazy. We had quite the time." He snorted, allowing a small smile. "Quite the time..." His mouth flattened suddenly inside his beard. "Until lanky here thought it would be a riot to lock an imp in the trunk."

My face flushed. "Yeah, sorry about that. Like James said, we have no memory of last night."

"Well, thanks to your little stunt, a whole gang of 'em waylaid me on my way home. Last thing I remember was an eyeball being shoved in my face. I woke up back there." He jerked a thumb toward the private room. "Don't know if it was the trying to bust out or being so ticked off, but it was getting awful hard to breathe in there." He pounded his chest with a fist. "Probably why I went a little berserk."

James and I exchanged a guarded look that said, *I won't mention Helga's suffocation spell if you don't.*

"Well, all's well that ends well," James chuckled. "Let's get you to Celestial Gardens."

Deputy Rollie had mentioned a kidnapping, and after the trunk incident, I assumed he'd meant Bolwig, but now Tjalf seemed the likelier candidate. As we recrossed the lobby, I asked him, "What's at the commune?"

"Left my war hammer behind."

James snapped his fingers and spun toward me. "Fantasia makes everyone hand over anything that carries the potential for violence before going inside her 'sacred space.' That must be where our stuff is!"

"I'll take that as a bonus," I said.

More than anything, we needed a solid lead on the case, which I hoped would also lead to Deputy Franks. Alive, preferably.

"I have a good feeling about this," James said.

I nodded, even though Tjalf was a walking, talking reminder that we couldn't get our hopes up too much.

"Hey, you guys mind swinging by Pauline's on the way?" the dwarf asked. "Haven't had anything to eat since last night, and I could go for another tray of those burgers."

20

Following our fourth meal of Pauline's in the last thirty-six hours, we left Grimstone proper and drove into the high desert. Beyond the Jeep's beams, mesas loomed across the moon-lit landscape. We passed under a sheer butte that I remembered from my first visit. As Tjalf polished off the last of his burgers, James turned the Jeep onto a dirt road. We climbed a good mile before leveling again.

"Full house tonight," James remarked.

I followed his nod to the car-filled lot we were coming on. Beyond, a field was populated by what looked like large yurts, several glowing with interior lights. As we parked and got out, I picked up a chorus of dreamy chants. It had to be after three a.m. Clearly people didn't come out here to sleep.

"Fantasia's is the big one." Tjalf nodded at a central dome that presided over the others.

He brushed off his sleeves and shirt as he took stomping lead, all business. James and I hustled to keep up. Before long, my ankle registered the first prick of a clinging spur, but I was more focused on the patterns of ley energy. James had called them "wild," and he wasn't wrong. Several lines terminated across the plateau in corkscrews and spraying whips, raising my guard. These kinds of spots tended to be strange attractors, explaining the commune and James's frequent visits for cleanup.

At the door to Fantasia's dome, Tjalf stopped.

"Sounds like she's got a ceremony going inside," he said. "We'd better wait."

I listened, but all I could make out was the soft murmur of astral music and occasional giggling. "How long do these things last?"

Tjalf shrugged. "Could go all night."

"Well, we don't have all night," I snapped.

It was annoying enough that we'd lost our memories because of this high priestess wannabe. But expecting us to wait around so she could indulge in whatever grandiose role she'd anointed herself was a bridge too far. Our business with her would take fifteen minutes, tops. She owed us that.

Stepping past Tjalf, I lifted the canvas flap and entered. Lamps glowed over a colorful assortment of pillows, mattresses, and blankets. Two dozen people were laid across them, dressed in pajamas and gowns and engaged in what, at first glance, looked like a clothed orgy. But they were just holding one another, and judging from their smiles and soft giggles, enjoying themselves thoroughly.

"Oh, no," Tjalf grunted as he and James arrived beside me.

The dwarf began to step back when a figure rose across the domed space. The svelte woman was dressed in an airy sleeveless caftan, her bronze arms vined in tattoos. Around a floral headdress her frizzy hair formed a near-perfect sphere.

She stared at us with intense cobalt eyes before her full lips softened into a smile.

"Welcome back, Dear Ones," she called serenely.

In her caftan, she seemed to float rather than walk over to us. She greeted us in turn, her body giving off a scent like smoking sage. When she squeezed my hands, I was surprised by the buzz of vitality.

"I know why you have come," she whispered. "I cannot abandon this space, however. I'm holding the energy." Her irises rolled back beneath her fluttering lashes. "Can you feel it?"

I did feel something: the warmth of contact and community. It had a pleasant, numbing effect, but it sat atop something more chaotic, as if the first were a fragile veneer and at any moment all hell could break loose.

"What kind of ceremony is this?" I asked.

Fantasia's irises returned. "Our Thursday night Cuddle Club."

"Okay..." I said. "We're just here to pick up some things we left last night and ask you a couple questions."

She smiled. "I'm going to encourage you to participate."

"Participate?" I said, looking over the room warily. "In this?"

"You entered our sacred space without asking permission. Your intrusion diluted the vibrational energy. Now it's incumbent on you to restore it. You owe this to the community." She somehow managed to sound pleasant and assertive at the same time, almost aggressively so. But I refused to back down.

"Look, lady. After the thirty-six hours we've had, we don't owe you jack squat."

I turned to James, who'd inspired me to stand up to Helga

and her minions, but he returned a sheepish grin. "Probably won't take too long," he said.

Dismissing him, I turned to Tjalf. Surely an ill-tempered dwarf wasn't going to put up with this, but there was zero resistance on his downcast face. He began grinding the toe of a shoe into the massive area rug.

I didn't believe it. He and James had the hots for Fantasia.

I sighed and squared my body toward her. "No," I said, pushing power into my wizard's voice. "There's a killer in Grimstone, and our friend is missing. I'm sorry, but we don't have time for this garbage."

The cooing and giggling inside the dome stopped, and I sensed the communal energy threatening to crack. Though Fantasia never stopped smiling, her eyes went icy, sending a frosty shiver through me. In my exasperation, I'd missed it: Fantasia was fae. Not full-blooded, but enough to be dangerous. And like a child holding a chainsaw, her control over her powers seemed shaky.

She stepped closer. "Now I really *must* insist."

As her cold aura swelled, I felt my own powers sputtering: a not-so-subtle threat. The surrounding murmurs grew into an angry chorus. Was this really worth fighting a pajama-clad mob over?

"Fine," I sighed.

Fantasia's eyes warmed again, the iciness dissipated, and cohesion returned to the dome. "Wonderful! Why don't you go to that side over there. There's just enough space for a three-spoon drawer."

"What's that?" I asked.

"I'll show you," James muttered.

"You comfortable?" James whispered to me.

"Hugging you and being cuddled by Tjalf? Not really."

The three of us were on a pile of cushions, me nestled behind James, an arm over his shoulder, and Tjalf doing the same to me, but with his stubby arm atop my waist. Fantasia had overseen our positioning to ensure there were no "energy-compromising gaps" between us before floating away to "hold space." By Tjalf's deepening breaths, it sounded as if he were falling asleep.

"How did I end up the middle spoon anyway?" I demanded.

"Just luck of the draw," James replied.

"Or maybe you've done this before?"

"Hey, Fantasia can be persuasive."

"You could have told me she was part-fae."

"I didn't mention that?"

"No. You didn't. Or that you're in love with her."

"Can you blame me?"

"Only if I ignore the fact that she's more dangerous than Loretta's snake."

"Yeah, well, Grimstone isn't New York with your four-million-plus females. I can't afford to be choosy." He went quiet for several seconds. "I wasn't entirely honest with you about something earlier."

"What?" I asked guardedly. I wasn't sure I could handle any more surprises.

"Remember when I told you how Lise left to live with her mother and how I said I was dealing?"

"Yeah?"

"I'm not." When his body began to shudder, it took me a moment to realize he was fighting back tears. "I know it was only a few weeks, but we got each other. I mean, I told her everything—all the way back to my first possession—and she didn't shy from any of it. It only made us tighter. I don't know if I've really loved a woman before, but I know I loved her. And if I could've gone with her, I would've."

He paused to sniffle and catch his breath.

Technically, I was already hugging him, so I lay there awkwardly. "My very first teacher, Lazlo, told me wizarding could be a lonely road," I said after a moment. "We have our powers, our obligations to our assigned places. But I've found that just as our magic alienates us, it also calls in certain people. The right people. If Allison is your right person, your magic will let you know."

He gripped my hand. "That's beautiful, man."

"And you were right about the insecure thing," I said.

"Huh?"

"I've been trying to prove to myself that I'm qualified to mentor you, and that's why I kept making those little flexes with my magic. I should've been bigger than that. I've clearly got some learning to do, too."

"You're being a little hard on yourself, Prof."

"After the last thirty-six hours? I'm not so sure."

"Man, I've watched the way you work, even through this. You take your responsibilities to this wizarding stuff seriously. If it wasn't for you, I might have said, 'screw it,' and taken off after Lise. The Order knows what it's doing. You're a good influence." He patted my hand. "I'm glad you're here."

I swallowed back my own emotions. "Thanks, bud."

The ceremony ended. Participants stood, exchanged parting hugs, and drifted out. James and I separated, but I had to nudge Tjalf awake. He snorted against my ribs and peered around. Realizing he was draped over me, he jerked back.

"Oh, I, ah, must've dozed off," he said with a nervous laugh.

By the time we'd all stood and stretched, Fantasia was beside us. "Wasn't that blissfully affirming?"

"It was kinda nice, actually," James said.

Tjalf grunted his agreement, but couldn't seem to look her in the eyes.

Fantasia brushed James's neck and stroked Tjalf's beard, turning the dwarf's cheeks the color of polished apples. She turned to me. "See what can happen when you say 'yes' to what you truly want?"

It wasn't as if she'd given me a choice, but I had to admit that I felt better than when we'd arrived. My confessional with James had helped, and he and I nodded at the other in acknowledgment.

"This way, Dear Ones."

We followed Fantasia from the main tent into a smaller adjunct. "Your belongings are inside," she said, opening a trunk engraved with neutralizing runes, several of them active. Between that and the wild patterns of ley energy out here, it was no wonder I hadn't been able to connect with my items.

Tjalf claimed his war hammer and James his wand and Peacemakers, kissing each grip in turn. I was tempted to do the same when I picked up my cane. I released the sword enough to see the top rune, for banishment, before slotting it back into its staff. From the back of the trunk, I lifted out my coin amulet and handed James his cross pendant. As I hung the coin around my neck, I smiled at the familiar hum of energy.

Remarkably, we'd found everything we had lost the night before.

Except for Franks, I reminded myself, dampening the glowy mood.

Fantasia sank onto a large beanbag, tucking her legs beside her, and gestured to the beanbags opposite her. From an end table, she lifted an absurdly slender pipe and began to smoke a strange-smelling herb.

"You have questions," she said as a wispy tendril circled her head.

James and I lowered ourselves. Tjalf, who needed a ride to his car, joined us, parking his massive hammer beside his bag.

"First, what did you give us last night?" I asked.

"That was a special concoction of tacote."

"Special, how? James and I lost our memories."

"As I warned you that you might," she said.

"And we agreed?"

"He did," she said, nodding at James.

My partner laughed awkwardly. "Guess we'll have to take your word for it. But it doesn't explain all the crazy stuff we got into. Getting married, kidnapping an imp, driving off in a pimpmobile?"

Fantasia's eyes narrowed through the smoke before illuminating again with a mirthful laugh. "Ahh, of course. I'd originally prepared the blend for a man who came to me because he couldn't say yes to anything. He didn't believe he was deserving, the poor soul. I designed the particular blend to release his spirit and fan his competitive fires. It's not something I normally encourage, but if you could have seen his timidity... Anyway, you insisted your need was urgent, and because a fresh preparation would have taken too long, I used what I had left over. With your consent, of course."

James and I exchanged a look. That combo of free-spiritedness and competitiveness accounted for just about everything we'd gotten up to last night. And it seemed we couldn't lay the blame at Fantasia's door.

"Okay," I exhaled. "We understand."

"And I can see it helped you work through some of your own issues?"

"Maybe," I allowed, "but we've still got a number that need resolving. What did we say we wanted last night?"

"A hidden name."

James and I turned to one another, the realization brow-smacking us at the same moment. The anonymous caller Marge had mentioned! The one who'd revealed the location of the four dying kids! Of course we would have gone after that info. It was the best lead in a case file bereft of them.

"Did we get it?" I asked.

"I believe you wrote it down."

I opened my notepad to the last page. "This? 'Swan Song'?"

"Is that how you wrote it?" She laughed. "The name I heard you speak was 'Swanson.'"

Apparently the drug had created some disconnect between my ear and hand. "'Swanson,'" I repeated.

Tjalf sat straighter. "Hey, I know a Swanson. Brunhold Realty sold them a house last summer, nice one too. The father is in metal commodities. He brought his punk-ass kid to the closing. Looked like a scowling rat."

"That's our anonymous caller," I said with certainty. "Do you remember the house?"

Tjalf nodded, but James stopped me from getting up.

"Since we're already here, why not use tacote to discover Franks's location?"

"I can do this," Fantasia said, setting her pipe aside. "But all I have on hand is last night's batch. Do you consent?"

"No," James and I blurted.

21

"Four more miles, then turn right on Pinyon," Tjalf called from the backseat.

The Jeep's frame shimmied as James pushed his ride to eighty. Usually not one for fast speeds, I would have been fine with a hundred now. It had taken us nearly two days, but we finally had a lead on the case—one we could remember.

"There's a good chance this'll lead us to Franks, too," I said. "If not, we'll go back to the sheriff's department. Now that I have my staff, I can cast a hunting spell on something of his."

James made a dubious face. "Hunting spells are no guarantee around here. Screwy ley lines. They're just as liable to send you to southeast Utah as your target, and I speak from experience."

"It worked on Taffy the last time," I pointed out.

"Yeah, because he's a dwarf. More energy to draw from."

"What worked on me?" Tjalf asked, shifting to the center of the backseat.

"Nothing," I said quickly before turning back to James.

"Then we'll better the odds by casting on something of Franks's that's really potent. Rollie's at the department, right? Let's put him on that."

James slowed enough for me to help manage the steering wheel while he pulled out his phone and called him.

"Sheriff's Department," Rollie answered over the speaker.

"Hey, it's Croft and Wesson," I said. "We—"

"Where's Franks?" he blurted out before I could continue. "You said you were bringing him back here."

"Yeah, he wasn't where we thought he'd be," I said, "but we're working on it."

"We are so screwed," he moaned.

"How so?" James asked.

"I finally talked to Sheriff Jackson—I couldn't keep ignoring her calls. I told her what Croft told me to say—that you're still out in the boonies—but she's suspicious. Said she's coming back early."

"How early?" I asked sickly.

"Eight if she stops for breakfast. Seven if she doesn't."

I checked my watch, then looked at James. That gave us less than three hours.

"She says she wants to prep Franks for the trial, but I'm telling you, she's suspicious."

"Stay cool, Rolls," James said. "We called because we need you to round up some of Franks's personal things."

"We need them to find him," I added to underscore their importance. "Anything with his hair or sweat—a hat, for example. Something of emotional significance works too, like an heirloom. Can you do that?"

"I-I'll try," he said.

He didn't sound sloshed now, just badly shaken.

"We'll be there soon," James told him, and ended the call.

"Will he deliver?" I asked.

James shrugged. "Fifty-fifty."

"Then let's find the perp."

At Pinyon Drive, James turned into a neighborhood overlooking Grimstone's south end. It featured resort-style homes, but I noticed most of them had FOR SALE signs, while half the lots hadn't been built out at all. Like in the rest of the country, Grimstone's real estate market was on life support. Tjalf barked out the turns until we were cruising down a street of partially-constructed homes.

"Swanson's is the last one," he said. "The only one we've finished down here."

At a cul-de-sac, James idled in front of a multi-level home surrounded by a ten-foot-tall security fence. An imposing gate stood at the foot of the driveway. He drummed his fingers over the steering wheel. "How are we gonna convince the parents to let us talk to their kid at four a.m.? Play the law-enforcement card?"

"Someone with that much money will play the lawyer card right back," I said.

Tjalf grunted in agreement. This was going to be more complicated than the bank heist. I was peering out my window in thought when, in the bones of the neighboring house, I spotted the orange point of a cigarette. When the slender shadow holding it caught me looking, it withdrew into the framing.

"Don't look now," I said, "but I think our anonymous caller is sneaking a smoke next door. Keep driving. I have an idea."

I shared my plan as James rolled back down the street and turned. When we were out of sight, I had him drop me off. For some reason, Tjalf hopped out too. As James returned back up the street, the dwarf and I paralleled him, hustling behind partial constructions until we were crouching at the edge of the one beside the smoker's hideout.

"I'll cover the other side," Tjalf panted.

That wasn't part of the plan, but I didn't want to argue after he'd guided us all the way out here. At the same time, I didn't want him blowing our chance. I pointed out the ravine that ran behind the lots.

"Make your way down there and around so he doesn't see you. Quietly, if possible."

Tjalf nodded and broke into a stomping run, carrying his massive war hammer like a lacrosse stick.

Over on the street, I heard James park the Jeep and get out.

"Swanson?" he called toward the construction site in a loud whisper. "I'm with the Grimstone County Sheriff's Department, but everything's cool. I just need to talk to you about what happened to your friends."

I figured James would either entice the kid out or prompt him to run. We just couldn't afford for him to escape back onto his secure property. I drew my cane into sword and staff to prevent that from happening.

Aiming the staff, I whispered, *"Protezione."*

After having to cast through my hand and a car antenna, the energy coursing down the wood was what I imagined cruising an open highway in a favorite car felt like. The air hardened around the home's rear framing in glints of light. A moment later, the smoker's shadow appeared, retreating from James's approach.

Has to be Swanson, I thought.

When he attempted to step between a pair of two-by-fours, he met my invocation. The cigarette fell in a splash of cinders. He felt along the invisible barrier, then attempted to slip out another way. I stood and walked toward him, shaping more walls of air to eliminate his exits and close him in.

We've got you, buddy.

We didn't want to hurt him, just contain him long enough to convince him we were the good guys. He began to dart back and forth like that poor mouse in Benny's cage. And then he dropped from sight.

What?

I rushed forward and onto the construction site, arriving at the spot at the same time as James. The kid had taken an unseen stairwell down, and now he was out back, running across a large pool area toward his house.

"Dammit," I grunted.

I raised my staff and James his wand, but a stocky shadow came charging from the ravine to head him off. The kid yelped in surprise and staggered back from Tjalf and his enchanted war hammer.

Before James or I could call him off, Tjalf brought the hammer down with a roar. The cracking contact of metal on concrete released a prodigious shockwave that sent the kid from his feet, and shook the entire site.

I grabbed onto James for balance as boards toppled around us. As the shockwave propagated into the distance, we raced down the steps and into the pool area. We arrived to find cracks still branching from a war hammer-sized crater, and the kid in the large, dug-out hole for the pool. A mound of dirt and sand had softened his landing, but the concussive wave had knocked him cold.

Tjalf scuffed up behind us with his hammer.

"Sorry about that," he grunted. "I'm used to battling other dwarves."

We jumped into the hole's shallow end, James calling light to his wand. The sprawled-out kid was dressed in shredded denim, a punk concert shirt showing between the flaps of his jacket. He sported an ink-black shag of spiky hair, but his face was uncannily smooth. When he blinked and stirred, I saw why.

Our anonymous caller was a girl.

I expected her to scream, but she only looked us over, a strange acceptance in her dark eyes.

I found my voice. "Are you okay?"

She appeared to have been more stunned than anything. Adjusting herself, she was soon perched on the dirt mound as though she'd meant to sit there, knees drawn in. She produced a pack of cigarettes from her jacket's breast pocket, lit one, and exhaled a long contrail like a seasoned smoker, though she couldn't have been more than seventeen. She stuffed the pack and lighter away.

"Depends," she said. "How much trouble am I in?"

"None," James assured her. "That's what I was trying to tell you."

"Then why did Warcraft over there just go full melee on me?"

Tjalf, who'd been swinging his hammer idly, moved it behind him. "I'm sorry. I was just... That is, I thought... I'll go stand over there." He hefted his hammer and climbed back out of the pool pit.

"Bitching beard, though," she said.

"First, are you Swanson?" I asked.

"What if I am?"

"Why the anonymous call?" James interjected. "Why not use your name?"

"I didn't think you guys were supposed to trace those," she

said, effectively confirming she was "Swan Song" and had placed the call. When James could be bothered, his interview game was top shelf.

"We're just trying to solve a case," he said, smiling agreeably.

She took another drag. "My parents." It took a moment for me to realize she was answering his question. "I didn't want them to know I'd snuck out again. That would've been strike eleven, and Dad's been threatening reform school."

"Ouch, been there, done that," James said. "He doesn't approve of your friends?"

"That's an understatement." She grunted a dead laugh. "But I guess that's not a problem anymore."

James took a seat on the mound beneath her. "We saw the photos. I'm really sorry."

My partner had the right read. This wasn't a barrage-her-with-questions-type situation. It called for empathy, and I could tell his was genuine. I stepped back to give them space.

"The crazy thing is, my dad might've saved my life," Swanson said.

James looked up at her. "Oh, yeah?"

"He was up later than usual, so I couldn't get the car out till after midnight. Torch had scored some weed, and we'd been going to an old farmhouse to smoke it. That night, I got there an hour late. By then, they were already sick. Bodies shriveling, hair falling out. I only recognized them from their clothes. Torch made a sound, but it was like when you're trying to scream in a dream." Her fingers shook as she took another drag. "I didn't know what to do. Didn't know how to help. So I grabbed the bag—I didn't want them getting in trouble, that's where my head was at—and called 9-1-1 from a burner."

"You smoked the bag before?" James asked.

"And since."

James and I exchanged a glance. Maybe Blecher was right and the culprit wasn't a drug.

"Could your friends have taken something else?" James asked. "Something stronger?"

She shook her head. "We weren't into that. And anyway, there wasn't anything else on them. I checked."

"Do you remember how they were positioned when you found them?" I asked.

Though she'd grown comfortable with James, she side-eyed me as if I were a narc. I was no doubt giving off intense vibes of concern. She was too young to be doing half of what she was describing, not least witnessing her friends' deaths. But I was starting to see a pattern, and I needed more info.

"He's cool," James told her.

"Torch, Blitz, and Queenie were on the back porch," she replied. "That's where we'd smoke. There was a killer view of the night sky over the field, and it was an easy spot to haul ass from if we had to."

"What about your other friend?" I asked.

"Moose was at the edge of the field, like he'd hopped down to take a leak. Big guy, but he had the bladder of an old lady."

"What kind of field are we talking?"

She shrugged. "Corn, maybe? It's been dead for a while."

My heart kicked into an uneasy gallop as I turned to James. "I think I know what we're dealing with. And if I'm right, we need to move now."

22

"A scarecrow?" James repeated for the third time. "Lanky-ass dude stuffed with straw and sporting a literal stick up his ass?"

"Sort of," I said, still organizing my thoughts.

We'd left the construction site after convincing Swanson to talk to someone about her experience. She didn't need to process that alone. Tjalf asked to come with us, muttering something about the family business being slow of late. He sat in the backseat, war hammer between his feet, as we sped into farm country.

"Some of the earliest scarecrows were beings made manifest through magic," I began. "In Germany especially, where they were called *bootzamon*—a version of the boogeyman. They scared birds away by rustling the stalks and making a knocking sound, like blocks of wood being clapped together. For the more persistent birds, the being sucked the life from them. Farmers would find their dried-out corpses all over the fields."

"Whoa."

"*Bootzamon* were hard to see, apparently, but they were described as men made of straw. The farmers who couldn't afford the magic started constructing their likenesses out of sticks and straw-stuffed clothes. The practice spread, becoming the modern-day scarecrow. But some of the old magic lingers in certain fields."

"How did it end up in this one?" James asked.

"If we dug through the property records, I'm sure we'd find a family name that goes back to Germany, but there's no time."

"You think the thing got resurrected and mistook a group of kids for birds?"

"I think the magic got infiltrated by something that feeds on human souls."

James snapped his fingers. "The holes."

He was referring to a recent attack by an ancient being who'd shredded the layers around our world. Until our Order could stitch the holes closed, we were more susceptible to visitors from other realms.

I nodded. "And the patterns of ley energy in Grimstone don't help. I've called them 'strange attractors.' In this case, I think they drew something on the nastier end of the spectrum. Possibly quasi-demonic."

"Okay, but what about the foreign compound in the kids' systems?"

"Transference. When a being like that drains a human of its life force, it sometimes leaves a little bit of itself behind. Magic from the *bootzamon* in this case. That's what you detected before the sample broke down."

"Damn." James blew out his breath. "If this thing just supercharged itself with four souls, how powerful are we talking?"

"Quite," I said. "But not enough to escape the cornfield, apparently. Not yet. If it had, more bodies would have turned up by now, I'm sure." That was a lucky break, considering our condition last night. "Though it bothers me that Swanson found three of her friends on the porch. That suggests a ranged attack."

"Is there a good way to kill it?"

"A *bootzamon's* weakness is fire," I said.

"And that'll take care of the quasi-demon dude too?"

"It's high-jacking the scarecrow's magic, so yeah. Without that, there'll be nothing to sustain it. To be safe, we'll have to burn the entire field and salt the earth, too. Purge it of any lingering *bootzamon* essence."

"Why not go straight to scorched earth? We've got enough dragon sand. Why deal with this thing at all?"

"Because Franks could be in there." I pictured the deputy, who lived out this way, stopping by the crime scene on his way home, walking the property, possibly venturing into the cornfield.

"Shit," James said.

"But nailing this scarecrow could be as easy as luring it to the field's edge. And since one of us is already resistant to magic…"

We both turned and looked at Tjalf.

"What?" he grunted.

The property was down an unmarked dirt road. Like most abandoned wood-frame farmhouses, this one had a haunted look about it—an effect enhanced by the low mist in the Jeep's approaching beams.

James peered around. "I don't see the deputy's car."

"Me neither," I said. "But this is Grimstone. If he left the keys inside, that's almost twenty-four hours for someone to have claimed it."

James turned the Jeep around and parked. The three of us got out and circled the house until we arrived beside the back porch Swanson had described. Beyond, several acres of cornfield rustled under a chilly breeze.

"You sure you're good with this?" I asked Tjalf.

"One hour," he reiterated. "Then I'll be ready to go home. Haven't had decent sleep in two days."

"Okay, then." I circled a finger. "Everyone in position."

Tjalf muttered as he stalked toward the edge of the cornfield. "Whole thing sounds like a load of hogwash anyway."

James and I climbed onto the porch. The old boards, littered with fragments of stalks and dried leaves, creaked underfoot. While he went inside to check out the house, I moved to a dark corner. Swanson had been right about the view. Beyond the field, a half-moon glowed above distant buttes and mesas. I could see why the kids had chosen this spot. Maybe it was my lack of sleep, but as I drew the shadows around me, I thought I could hear ghostlike conversations and the laughter of young friends. I heard screams, too.

With burning eyes, I scanned the field for the killer.

James returned shortly. "Inside's clear," he whispered.

He took his position at the other end of the porch and melded into the shadows. Tjalf had reached the cornfield, and he paced the boundary, swinging his war hammer beside him like a pendulum. He started into a harsh, dwarfish tune. If the scarecrow hadn't known he was here before, he did now.

But five minutes became ten and then thirty.

I was shifting to revive my tingling right foot when the corn stalks rustled. The expected breeze never reached me. All appeared still. The next rustle was accompanied by the sound of clapping blocks.

I straightened, my heart in my throat. I could see it now. Something was moving through the stalks, heading in our general direction. I got James's attention to make sure he saw it too. Our gazes dropped to Tjalf.

He'd stopped pacing and was facing the field, surely close enough to hear the noise. But his arms remained lax at his sides.

With his long beard acting as a screen, it took me a moment to see that the leather-bound handle of his parked war hammer was supporting his chin. He'd somehow managed to fall asleep standing up. The knocks sounded again as the line of rustling veered toward him.

"Tjalf!" I shouted.

23

James and I jumped down from the porch, magic crackling around my sword and his wand.

"*Tjalf!*" we shouted again.

Dwarves might have been resistant to magic, but it helped if they were conscious. The plan was for him to hit the scarecrow with a dose of dragon sand that I would ignite. Sound, but once again, only if Tjalf were awake. While James continued shouting his name, I switched to instructions.

"The sand! Ready the dragon sand!"

The sound of rustling and clapping blocks grew until it was nearly on top of Tjalf. Dammit, I was going to have to cast a protection, spoiling our element of surprise.

But then the dwarf came to with a snorting "Humprf?" He shook his head. "What in the—"

We'd needed the scarecrow to manifest in order to destroy it. We got our wish now as a gangly shadow lunged from the field.

But instead of throwing the sand we'd packaged for him, Tjalf resorted to his warring instincts. With speed belying his stockiness, he hefted his hammer and brought it around in a whooshing arc. Blue light flashed as enchanted iron met *bootzamon* magic. Tjalf completed his swing and staggered back, dead leaves and stalks raining down.

James and I arrived on either side of him as the field fell silent. No more rustling or clapping.

Tjalf propped his hammer against a shoulder and puffed out his barrel chest. "Well, I guess that settles that."

I opened my wizard's senses. "The scarecrow wasn't destroyed," I said, "just scattered."

"Does that give us time to find Franks before we burn and salt this place?" James asked.

The question had no sooner left his mouth than the field swarmed us. I swore as stalks and leaves lashed my body and face. I tried to parry them with my sword and staff before slotting the first inside the second and groping around the thrashing storm with my free hand. I found a muscular forearm and gripped it.

"Where's Tjalf!" I shouted.

"I've got him!" James shouted back.

I summoned power and released it with a Word: *"Protezione!"*

Light pulsed from the opal inset in the end of my raised cane and hardened into a protective dome around us. I pushed the dome out, breaking and flattening stalks, until it stalemated against the *bootzamon* magic. The three of us released one another, Tjalf panting beneath his raised hammer, his ginger beard littered with debris.

The field continued to thrash on all sides.

"Where in the hell are we?" James asked, releasing his Peacemakers from their hip holsters.

"We haven't moved," I said. "The thing may not be strong

enough to break from the field, but it can bring the field to its victims." That explained the debris I'd seen on the porch. "It wants to separate us."

"Then drop the shield and let it try!" Tjalf thundered.

But I kept the shield up. We were on the scarecrow's turf. Did we clear out and regroup? Or did we somehow turn this to our advantage?

James flinched back as a large face took form in the dead vegetation. It looked like a rotting sack, gray leaves crowding its open mouth and pits for eyes. It was there for a second before disappearing.

"Damn, that's fugly," James muttered.

His cross and my coin pendant glowed with protective magic.

The scarecrow's face reappeared to my right, cinder-like points smoldering inside its pits now. We were glimpsing the quasi-demonic being that had latched onto the *bootzamon* magic. A deep rattling sounded, like a hungry breath. The face scowled at the shield before withdrawing into the corn stalks again.

Tjalf grunted and prepared his hammer as the scarecrow manifested on the other side of us.

Maybe it was my imagination, but I sensed the being probing our powers, exploring for weaknesses. Using my wizard's senses, I reciprocated. Every time the scarecrow disappeared, the *bootzamon* magic dispersed over the field, and every time it reappeared, the magic gathered into the nightmarish face.

"Move behind me," I whispered to the others.

Reaching into a pocket, I thumbed open a vial of dragon sand. If I was a quick enough draw, I could light this manifested sucker up and destroy it. As James and Tjalf stepped back, I moved forward. The scarecrow's smoldering eyes canted down to the hand in my pocket and withdrew into the corn again.

I followed the *bootzamon* magic as it dispersed, then turned toward where it was gathering again. I readied the dragon sand, but instead of a scarecrow reappearing, a loud rattle sounded, like a forceful expulsion of air. A torrent of objects flew in, battering my shield. It took me a moment to understand they were birds. More accurately, the *ghosts* of birds the scarecrow had sucked dry over the years.

Unsurprisingly, most were crows.

They flew from the stalks in a torrent, hammering my shield and gathering over it in a growing swarm. I staggered, as much from the onslaught of talons and beaks as from the effort to channel more energy into our shield. Tjalf alternately covered his head and readied his hammer as the dome wobbled.

"How you doing, Prof?" James asked.

"Not great."

I was wincing with every sharp strike, my struggle to uphold the protection becoming more painful and desperate. The attack was psychic as much as physical. Sparks spilled from the dome in a growing shower. Before it could fail entirely, I fed it power from my coin pendant and shouted, "*Respingere!*"

The shield blew out in a release of force and bluish light, scattering the ghost birds into mist and flattening corn stalks for a good twenty feet. I blinked in the sudden exposure, adjusting my grip on sword and staff.

"Let's get out and regroup," I said.

"Yeah, no argument here," James breathed.

I oriented toward where I believed the farmhouse was

and aimed my sword. With an invocation, I opened a swath. I'd been slightly off the mark, but there was the edge of the yard, glowing dimly in the half-moon.

"Stay together," I said, my warning buried by James's gunshots.

I wheeled just as the scarecrow's face dispersed from the salt rounds. By the time I turned back, the swath I'd created was gone. The stalks pressed in again. Tjalf swung his war hammer, narrowly missing the scarecrow's next ghastly appearance. Some baddies liked to play games with their victims, but this thing's hunger was palpable.

Its sole aim was to consume us.

James swore as a tendril of crackling vegetation wrapped his leg. I slashed my sword, hacking him free. More stalks wrapped my neck and yanked me into a gargling backpedal. Tjalf brought his hammer down with an angry shout, scattering them.

"Thanks," I rasped.

"He's going guerilla warfare on us," James said.

That was a good term for it. The scarecrow was coming in and out so fast, using hit and run tactics, there was no time to target it with the dragon sand, much less ignite it. If we didn't adapt *our* tactics, we were going to exhaust our energy, and I'd already expended enough trying to sustain the shield.

"You know that polygamy bond?" I called to James.

"What about it?"

"Well, it ties us to Loretta but also to one another."

"Whoa, hold on a second. Are you saying you and me are married?"

"As far as the bond is concerned... sort of?"

"Man, I did *not* need to know that right now."

He stopped to shoot another mass of grasping stalks, the salt rounds temporarily scattering the magic.

"Listen, it just means we're energetically connected," I said. "But we can use that. The scarecrow is going to keep popping in and out like this, but if it wants to feed, it's going to have to focus. That will make it vulnerable."

"A little help?" Tjalf grunted.

I turned to find him struggling with several stalks looping his arms. James covered me while I hacked Tjalf free. The dwarf swung his hammer in an air-bending arc as if to warn away the other corn plants.

"What does that have to do with the polygamy bond?" James asked.

"I'm going to offer myself. When the scarecrow manifests to feed, I need you to use the bond to find me and destroy it." I drew the vial of dragon sand from my pocket and passed it to him. "And be quick, please."

He blocked my hand. "I'll go."

"What?"

"You may be lucky, but I'm the gambler in this marriage."

"James, all you have to do is find me." I focused into the powerful band that connected us to Loretta—and each other—until it shimmered into a distinct note. "Do you feel that? When I go in, follow it. I'll keep the scarecrow off me until I see you."

"Just let me do it, Prof. I trust you to find me more than I trust me to find you."

He opened up with both revolvers, creating a narrow path in the animated stalks. Before I could stop him, he plunged inside.

"Hey!" I called, then swore.

The cornfield around Tjalf and me shivered to a rest. In

my wizard's vision I watched the *bootzamon* magic contract. It veered toward James in a hungry line of rustling and clapping, anticipating its meal.

Though the stalks had closed in James's wake, I had a lead blocker in Tjalf. With dwarfish power radiating from his hammer, he bellowed and charged forward. I hunkered behind him, and we plunged into the parting stalks like a fullback and tailback surging for the end zone. Concentrating into the polygamy bond, I used Tjalf's thick shoulder to guide him in the right direction.

At last, we broke into a small clearing, where James was firing the last of his ammo into the looming scarecrow. Holstering his revolvers, he stepped around so the scarecrow's back was to us, then popped its sack head with a pair of left jabs.

"You ain't so bad," he goaded, shuffling his feet.

Never having been punched before—or taunted—the scarecrow recoiled. I launched the vial of dragon sand with a force invocation. It struck the center of the scarecrow's back, scattering the granules.

Bullseye.

But before I could release the sand's thermal energy, the scarecrow lunged, burying James in a mound of dead corn plants.

Dammit.

The dragon sand was exactly where I wanted it, but I couldn't torch the scarecrow without burning James. We were talking about a five thousand-degree inferno. My partner's shouts became muffled, replaced by a long, rattling breath.

The scarecrow was inhaling James's soul.

As I ran toward them, I felt the effect through the bond. It was a ghastly feeling, like a vagrant's blood turning to ice behind a dumpster. And the being who'd hijacked the *bootzamon* magic was enjoying it.

If I can't burn you, I thought fiercely, *I can banish you.*

I drew my sword as I arrived at the mound. The blade's first rune, the one for banishment, was already glowing. The rattling paused, as if in question, and I plunged the blade into the being's side.

A fierce gasp sounded.

"Disfare!" I shouted.

Light erupted from the rune in a small nova, tearing through the scarecrow mound, and launching me onto my back. A fiendish scream rose and echoed out, and then debris was falling all around me.

I sat up and blinked away the blinding afterimage. Tjalf, who'd rolled off a short distance, swore as he dusted himself off and collected his hammer.

I spotted James across the clearing, down on his side. I ran over, brushed stalks and leaves off him, and pulled him onto his back. Terrified I'd find a withered mask staring up at me, I snorted in relief at the sight of his youthful face wincing and spitting out dried corn silk as his cross pendant dimmed.

"Dude... I think that thing tried to tongue me."

He was fine.

24

We searched the entire field using various magics as well as old-fashioned footwork, but there was no sign of Franks. Following a second sweep to make absolutely sure, we lit the field up with dragon sand.

While I contained the fire, James drove into town for salt. He returned with several sacks of the road variety, which we scattered over the field. Possibly feeling guilty for falling asleep, Tjalf pitched in. The salt dissolved the final pockets of *bootzamon* energy from the smoldering soil until none remained.

Tjalf dusted off his hands. "Can I get that ride now? I'm ready for a bath and a bed."

The pinkening sky revealed how soot-covered we all were, not to mention exhausted. I checked my watch. After six a.m. The dwarves' compound was at the other end of the county, but even if we went straight to the sheriff's department, prepared a hunting spell, and locked onto Franks (a big *if*), by the time we recovered him, Marge would have been back long enough for second breakfast.

I shrugged at James. His call.

"Yeah, might as well," he sighed.

We drove in silence as the sky paled and Sheriff Jackson's truck drew ever closer to Grimstone. Tjalf directed us to where his yellow Hummer had run off the road and into some creosote bushes when the imps waylaid him.

"It was good hanging with you, Tjalf," James said as he pulled over. "You're a solid dude."

"Yeah, thanks for everything," I added, twisting around to face him. "*Despite* everything we got you into."

James and I offered our hands, but dwarves weren't known for their decorum. Returning a terse grunt, he hopped from the Jeep with his hammer and dragged it toward his vehicle. James waited to ensure the engine would start.

"That Taffy is all right," he said as the dwarf backed onto the road and drove off in a plume of dust. "Too bad he'll go right back to being a grumpy ass the next time we see him."

"Really?"

"It's already happened with me a couple times."

"Well, at least we know he has a weakness for burgers." I nodded at the center console, where James had placed his phone. "Should I call her, or do you want to?"

His smile shrank. "Marge?"

"She thinks Franks is going to be waiting for her when she arrives. I'm with you now on coming clean."

"A little late, don't you think?"

"Better late than too late."

The phone rang. I reached for it, but James grabbed it first.

"Hello?" he answered warily. His face brightened. "Oh, hey!"

He pivoted the phone back and mouthed, *Loretta.*

Oh, crap, I thought. *We still have our polygamy bond to deal with...*

"Yeah, yeah, we're fine," he said. "Those guys? Oh, just a big misunderstanding. We got it all sorted out."

And the favor we were supposed to have done for Blecher, the vulture shifter...

"Well, after that we ran into an old friend—more like she ran into us—but she needed our help on an errand."

Not to mention whatever we stole from the bank vault for Helga.

"After that? We got a tip on a case we're working. And get this, we just solved the thing!"

Yeah, at least we took care of that.

"Okay, see you soon, hon." He made a kissing sound before dropping the phone back into the console.

"Was that last part really necessary?" I asked.

"Our wife didn't sound happy about us being gone so long, and I didn't want her taking it out on my dog." He wheeled the Jeep around. "Mind if we go there now? It's on the way, and I want to grab Annie."

"Sure. Why not."

"I'll make you a deal," James said as he pulled into the parking lot of Mesa Park Apartments. "I'll go up and deal with Loretta, if you stay and call Marge. Coming clean will sound better coming from you."

"You said the same thing yesterday about me bullshitting her."

"Well, Marge is a special case. Between the two of us, *everything* is going to sound better coming from you."

"I have a feeling that's about to change." I sighed. "Give me the phone."

James entered her number and handed it over. "Just hit the green button when you're ready."

We got out of the Jeep, but while James hurried up the steps, I paced the length of the lot, weighing the options. Did I blur the timeline to make it sound as if we really *had* been out in the boonies for the last two days? Or did I start from the beginning and tell her everything? I mean, it wasn't our fault we'd blacked out. Not entirely.

As Annie greeted James with an enthusiastic bout of barking, I studied the green button. Not ready to press it, I paced the lot again.

Amid the chaos of the past day and night, I'd learned something valuable. This mentoring job was a two-way street: James was helping me as much as I was helping him. Probably what the Order had intended. And the way we'd handled the scarecrow? We'd team-worked the crap out of that sucker, sparing untold victims.

On the other hand, we'd quite possibly sacrificed the one that mattered most to Marge, her deputy, and I feared she was going to outlaw me from Grimstone County. At one time I would have welcomed it—a good excuse to stay in New York—but I'd be bummed not to be able to work with James again.

"Screw it," I decided, hitting the green button.

I was still supposed to be the responsible one. I would tell her everything and let the chips fall where they would.

The line intoned twice before she answered. "Wesson," she said sharply.

"It's Croft, actually, but I'm calling for both of us. Are you back in town?"

"An hour out. Where the hell have you been?"

"Yeah, listen, uh..." I took a breath and peered toward the baby blue sky. "We screwed up."

"What are you talking about?"

"The case, the last two days... Things got out of hand, and we lost Franks."

"What?"

"We can't find Franks."

"I don't know what kind of game you're playing, Croft, but he's due in court in three hours."

"Yeah, that's probably not gonna hap—"

Something nailed me in the side of the head. I reeled, dropping the phone. James hurtled the upstairs railing and landed beside me, scattering the remnants of his energy bolt. He pawed for the phone and picked it up.

"Sheriff, it's James," he said quickly. "Don't mind Everson—poor guy hasn't slept in two days. There was a little mix up, but Franks is fine. He'll be waiting when you get here. Oh, and we solved the case. We'll tell you all about it when we're face-to-face. Sorry to run, but we've got a couple things to tie up. See you soon."

He ended the call.

"What the *hell*?" I said, rubbing my scorched ear.

"Sorry, man, I was aiming for the phone." He grabbed my arm. "C'mon, Loretta has something you need to hear."

Annie, whom he'd secured to the upstairs railing, barked and tongue-lapped my legs as I staggered past her in James's grip. Outside the apartment door, James paused and passed a hand over his face, turning it somber. Though still confused, I mirrored the look. Inside, Loretta was sitting on the floor in the middle of the living room, staring listlessly at Benny in his cage. She was wearing a similar robe as yesterday morning, but this one was deep black, as if she were in mourning.

James cleared his throat. "Croft needs to hear this, too."

Without looking up, she said, "I want the annulment."

I stared at her in disbelief.

"Now tell him the reason," James said.

I raised a finger. "Could you hold that thought?"

I drew a tube of copper filings from my coat, sprinkled a large circle around Loretta, then jerked my head for James to join me. We knelt in front of her and took her hand in ours, thumbs on the ring's ingot. Even with the bond thrumming between the three of us, Loretta's eyes remained downcast and her hand limp. I was rushing this, but I didn't want her second-guessing whatever had brought her to her decision. I closed the circle with a Word, then posed the crucial question, first in an archaic language, then English:

"Do the bonded three agree to this dissolution?"

"Yes," I said, answering myself.

"Yes," James echoed.

We both peered warily at Loretta. "Yeah," she agreed at last.

"Then the marriage is dissolved," I announced, trying my hardest not to smile. *"Disfare."*

The bonding energy explored the three of us, as if to confirm our decision. It then pulsed from my grandfather's ring, shrank to a point, and disappeared entirely. Loretta drew her hand away, and the loose ring slid into my waiting palm.

"Is that it?" she said, looking up.

"That's it," I said, trying—and failing—to sound saddened as I slotted the ring onto my own finger.

Hallelujah!

Loretta stood and hunched her shoulders several times,

then twisted her hips back and forth. I had no idea what she was doing until her lips pulled from her front teeth. Was that a... smile?

"Holy crap, that feels better," she breathed, answering my question. "Anyone else want a shot of Johnnie Walker to celebrate?"

Despite my profound confusion, I raised my hand. All that mattered was that she'd released us from the polygamy bond, and I had my grandfather's ring back. If anything, that called for the whole bottle. But before Loretta could hustle off to the kitchen, James stepped in front of her.

"First, tell Croft the reason," he said. "He deserves that much."

Loretta's teeth disappeared as she turned toward me. "Like I told James, it was the way you two left me here yesterday."

"When the armed men took us away?" I asked.

"And how many times did I say I wanted to come? But you ignored me. Told me to stay put, like a dog. The day after our wedding, no less. So I had a good talk with Benny and Annie, and we all agreed that not being included was worse than being alone, and I'd be a stupid-head to think it was going to get better. I didn't sleep a wink last night. The more I thought about it, the heavier that ring weighed on me."

I nodded in a show of sympathy while saying a silent prayer of thanks to Blecher and the vulture shifters.

"And it wasn't just that," she continued. "The way you kept trying to one-up each other? At first it was kinda hot—and it did get me married—but you never stopped. I was trying to be a wife, not a mama to a couple of grown men. Even at our party at the sheriff's department you wouldn't quit."

"Tell him how," James prompted.

"You kept betting Jam-Jam he couldn't stick a car up on one of those buttes. That's when I remembered I'd left my check at the diner, but the two of you were too busy squabbling to even offer me a lift."

I knew exactly which butte I would have meant—and whose car. I stared at James, who was nodding fervently.

"There's still time," he said.

25

The sheer butte we'd passed on the way to and from Celestial Gardens loomed over the road ahead, its top catching the sunlight above the mesas. It was small for a butte, its rock sides rising only fifty feet before ending at a flat top.

Flat enough to place a car.

"Do you think you pulled it off?" I asked James.

"Oh, I *know* I pulled it off. How do you think I ended up with these?" He gestured to the wounds on his face as well as the burn line in his hair. "Clearly you wanted the last word on who's the superior wizard."

"What? Nah..."

But then I remembered the trashed condition of the breakroom and the smell of ozone. Hopped up on Fantasia's special tacote concoction, I must have challenged James to a wizard duel when we'd returned.

"Oh, man. I am so sorry."

"Have you seen yourself? I gave at least as good as I got, and if I didn't, that fresh burn on your ear makes us even."

"Still," I said, touching my sore lobe. "I owe you a huge apology."

"We already hugged it out at Fantasia's, but I wouldn't mind some healing magic later."

"Done. And if I'm not banished from Grimstone after this, I'll stick around to help get your trailer back in order."

"Right on, but first let's grab Franks's lanky butt."

I nodded, thinking how we'd just resolved most of the five-to-eight a.m. gap on our timeline.

James pulled off the road and onto a dirt track that circled the butte. We got out and, with necks craned, began calling for Franks. Annie howled from the Jeep. When no head appeared over the butte's edge, I backed up.

"What are you doing?" James asked.

"Getting a running start," I said, gripping my cane tightly. "Be ready to catch me if I fall short."

Without saying it, I was telling him I trusted him. James nodded, silver light already swimming around the end of his wand. When I was a good sixty feet back, I took off toward the butte, shoes kicking up sand.

Aiming my cane down and slightly back, I shouted, *"Forza dura!"*

In a blast, the force invocation launched me like a catapult. The arc looked good, the force sufficient. The butte's wall sped past until I was above the crest and looking down at a green-on-white cruiser parked squarely in its center.

Hell yes!

I called another invocation to slow my descent. I landed hard anyway, rolling over stone and brush until I was sprawled beside the cruiser's rear fender. I got up and pawed around to the driver's door. When I didn't see anyone inside, I panicked. But Franks was curled up in the backseat, using his coat as a blanket.

"He's here!" I called elatedly.

"He all right?" James called back.

I opened the door and shook his legs. "Franks?"

He stirred and peered at me over a narrow shoulder. "Croft?" he rasped.

His eyes were puffy and his lips cracked, but nothing some healing magic and hydration couldn't fix. I'd been annoyed when Marge had assigned him to shadow us, but now I could have bear-hugged the man.

"You're safe, buddy," I told him.

"How the heck did I even get up here?"

"He's good!" I shouted to James.

"Then let's go!" he called. "Get in and drive the cruiser off the side facing the road. I'll catch you."

"What?" The thought alone made my stomach invert. "You sure?"

"Hey, I got it up there, didn't I?"

I swaddled Franks in healing magic and buckled him in where he lay. I then climbed into the driver's seat. The key was already in the ignition, but the battery was dead. The lights must have been on when we'd stuck him up here. I slotted the gear stick into neutral, buckled myself in, but left my door open.

"Ready?" I called.

"Ready!" James answered.

Aiming my cane outside, I used small force blasts to roll, then nudge us to the edge of the butte. I attempted a steadying breath, but my heart was racing too fast. It was one thing to trust James to spot me on the way up, but trusting him to catch a four-thousand-pound vehicle with two of us inside?

"Ready?" I called again.

"Stop stalling, Prof! I've got you!"

I supposed I owed him that trust for the scarecrow.

"All right," I whispered, then counted down for him to hear. "Three... two... *one!*"

My next blast was a big one. I retracted my cane and slammed the door closed as the front of the cruiser dipped. In the next moment, the entire vehicle was plunging off the butte. Open sky became onrushing desert. I could see James standing near the Jeep and could hear Annie barking. Seizing the steering wheel, I uttered a prayer so profanity-laced that it could only defeat the purpose.

And then we were bobbing, the cruiser suspended in a net of James's silver energy. He lowered us the rest of the way down.

I staggered out, weak-kneed. "Nice going, man."

"Dude, that was badass!" he exclaimed, running toward us.

When he arrived, I held up a handful of folders. "Look what slid out from under the passenger seat."

James laughed. "Deputy *and* case file? Now that's a two-fer!" He knocked on the back window and popped his thumb up at Franks. Under the influence of my healing magic, the deputy could only peer back at him blearily.

"I'd offer to try driving this back," I said of the cruiser, "but the battery's dead."

"Can you steer and brake?"

I nodded.

"Good, 'cause I don't have jumpers, but I've got a towing cable. How we doing for time?"

I checked my watch. "Thirty-two minutes ago Marge said she was an hour out."

Following the wildest tow job the county had ever seen, I burst into the sheriff's department, holding doors open for James, who was carrying Franks. Annie ran excited circles around us. In the breakroom, I righted the couch, and James lowered Franks onto the plaid cushions. The deputy already looked better, my healing magic having restored the contours of his puffy face. His relative youth helped.

Deputy Rollie ran in and blinked. "Where did you find him?"

"That's not important right now," James said. "Marge will be here in fifteen. Do everything we say, and you just might keep your job. First, go in the bathroom and soak a couple hand towels in cold water. Put one on his head and have him suck on the other one. We need to get fluids in him. When he's awake enough, I want him sipping from a bottle. Try to get a liter down his chicken gullet."

I was impressed as much by James taking command as Rollie's response. As if brushed by an electric fence, the senior deputy skipped into action. I checked my watch, then looked at the scored walls and the field of crushed beer cans.

"Think we can clean this entire place in time?"

"Let me worry about that." James drew his wand. "Get started on the case report."

Despite the circumstances, I bit back a proud smile. He was starting to sound like me.

In the conference room, I sat in the same chair I'd used for the briefing two nights earlier. Hunched over the special form Marge had designed for supernatural cases, I outlined the steps we'd taken, from exhausting the leads in the case file, to discovering the identity of the anonymous caller, to connecting her account to an old legend, to eradicating the killer and preventing his return.

I conveniently "forgot" to put in dates and times.

I was wrapping up the summary portion when I heard the main door to the department open, followed by a familiar limping cadence. I dotted the final period as the footsteps stopped in the doorway to the conference room. I looked up to find Sheriff Jackson regarding me with her flinty eyes.

"Oh, hey," I said. "I was just finishing our report."

I placed the form neatly on top of the other documents and slid the entire file toward her.

Wordlessly, she lowered herself onto a chair and began skimming. "A *bootzamon*, huh," she said at last.

"Yeah, craziest thing." To buy James and Deputy Franks time, I went into excessive detail about how the compound had ended up in the victims' systems and why it was natural to have mistaken it for a drug.

"And the perp was at the farmhouse?" she cut in.

"That's right. In that old cornfield out back."

As she studied my eyes, I could see her trying to calculate how well my report lined up with the message I'd left her yesterday afternoon about us being out of communication. She started to talk, but James came running in. It looked as if he had something to tell me, but upon seeing Marge, he changed tact.

"Sheriff!" he exclaimed. "You made it!"

"I made it," she repeated, stiffening as he hugged her from behind.

"I see Croft's gone over the case with you," he said, joining me across from her. "So?"

"So what?" she said.

"Remember our deal?"

"*Your* deal, you mean? If this is all accurate"—she tapped the case file—"I owe you an apology. Seems it had nothing to do with a new dealer stepping into Santana's vacuum. Just some damned scarecrow."

He chuckled graciously and waved a hand. "Bygones."

She fake-chuckled along with him before her lips drew suddenly against her teeth. "Now do you want to explain that phone call I got an hour ago?" she said. "About screwing up and losing my deputy?"

I'd been afraid that was incoming, but before I could respond, James leaned forward.

"That was my fault, Sheriff. Croft and I have been picking at each other since we started this case. I thought it would be funny to convince him I'd lost Franks. The prank went a little too far, and he called you."

"Is that so," she said, her gaze shifting to me.

"I honestly thought we'd lost him," I said. Not a lie.

"It was juvenile," James admitted. "But you know me."

"Where is he?"

James cocked his head. "Chilling in the breakroom."

Marge pushed herself from the table and headed there, James and I close at her heels. When she pulled the door open, the breakroom was back to its former state—no crushed beer cans or obvious damage.

Better yet, Franks was sitting up on the couch, fraternizing with Rollie. In his fresh deputy shirt and combed-over hair, he looked miles better than me and James. And here I'd just been hoping the guy was awake. As he sipped from a water bottle he'd been dangling between his knees, he noticed Marge.

"Hey, Sheriff!" he said, wiping his mouth. "Are you ready for me?"

She looked at him, then around the room. Annie, who had laid down in a corner, lowered her thick head to her paws and watched Marge warily. The same anxiety brewed in my gut, but not from a fear of being thumped on the nose. I hadn't known Marge long, but I knew she didn't miss many details.

"Yeah," she replied slowly. "Let's head to the courthouse. We'll use one of their offices to go over your testimony." She turned to Rollie and scowled, "Think you can handle dispatch today?" She was miffed he'd blown his assignment of keeping tabs on Franks while he kept tabs on us.

"Yes, Sheriff." He left the room, appearing more relieved than chastened.

She waved Franks out, too. As he strutted past her, Marge wheeled toward us on her prosthetic leg. "As for the two of you..."

I swallowed dryly. Was this where she revealed that she'd known all along what we'd gotten up to?

"Go home and get some rest. You look like shit."

"Yes, ma'am," James said.

"Yes, ma'am," I echoed.

As she left the breakroom, James balled up the shoulder of my coat excitedly. He waited until Marge's limping footsteps had faded before pulling a folded piece of paper from the back of his pants.

"What's this?" I asked.

"I found it on the ground out back when I was taking out the garbage. It's the favor we did Blecher."

"No way," I whispered as he unfolded it.

"It had to do with a stupid traffic ticket Rolls gave him. Eight over the limit in the middle of nowhere." He laughed. "We must have gotten Franks to delete it from the system, and this is the printed proof for Blecher."

"It was only a hundred dollars," I read in confusion.

James shrugged. "Maybe Blecher was facing license suspension, and we know how much he loves that unholy ride of his."

When the door to the breakroom opened again, James was almost too slow to sleight-of-hand the evidence behind his forearm. Marge reappeared, adjusting her cowboy-style sheriff's hat on her head.

"One more thing," she said.

James and I waited anxiously as she tongue-probed a back tooth. At last, her knotted lips relaxed into a smile.

"Nice job."

26

James and I followed Sheriff Jackson's order and slept for two days. Part of it was the healing magic I'd administered to James and myself, but mostly it was the sheer exhaustion of everything we'd gone through.

On the morning of the third day, we woke up feeling more or less ourselves. Our wounds had healed, and James's hair was even beginning to grow back in the burn groove my magic had inflicted.

Around noon, Deputy Rollie stopped by with a to-go bag —steak tacos, for a change—our reward for helping him keep his job. Life under Sheriff Jackson's thumb had returned to normal, he said. While she carried some suspicion around exactly what transpired while she'd been away, she didn't press the issue. She was more than happy to file the quadruple homicide in the "solved" cabinet in order to focus on a backlog of mundane cases, not to mention her ongoing administrative duties.

Before Rollie drove off, he renewed the vow of secrecy

he'd made to James, and said Deputy Franks would do the same.

There was no telling why, but poor Franks had been under the influence of the tacote plant as well that night. He remembered nothing before awakening atop the butte the next morning, his head pounding. With no cell, radio, or satellite signal, he'd shouted himself hoarse that first day and then waved his service flashlight at the occasional passing car that night, only to be ignored, including by us. Weak and dehydrated, he'd just about given up by the time we realized what we'd done.

James and I didn't know if we'd intended for him to go onto the butte with his cruiser—I certainly hoped not—but we promised to make it up to him.

I submitted my report to the Order, including damages, and a flatbed truck arrived that week with a new bedroom component for James's trailer. A man of my word, I stayed to help him, and together we hauled off the wreckage, reset the home on its foundation, and installed the new addition. The job took us three full days, even with magic, and that didn't include re-warding the home, which took another two.

It wasn't easy, especially in the heat of the day, but it *was* nice being able to collaborate on something that didn't involve imminent life or death.

James and I spent the evenings in lawn chairs out back, sipping beers and recounting the events around the case as if they were already legend. The blackout, the jailbreak, the pimpmobile, our marriage to Loretta, the bank heist, finding Tjalf instead of Franks, the frigging cuddle session. What *hadn't* we done in those two days?

One question that remained was the safety deposit box. The

theft never made the news, and James was prepared to let it go, but I browbeat him into putting out some discreet inquiries. We owed someone for whatever we'd taken. A young librarian named Myrtle, whose expertise was Grimstone history, called back with an answer. I picked up what I could on James's end. My last time here he'd been crushing hard on Myrtle, but now he mostly listened, seeming to confirm he wasn't over Allison.

"You're not going to believe this," he said as he pocketed his new phone.

We were in his backyard again, a meteor shower just kicking off overhead.

"What?"

"The box belonged to Helga."

"The box she had us steal? Get outta here."

"Number ninety-two," he confirmed. "Myrtle says it's been in her name for the last century, along with half the other boxes in there." He paused to sip his beer. "So was Helga just screwing with us?"

"Or too lazy to go down there and withdraw it herself."

"That *witch*," he seethed. "And now she's got my gold nugget."

"They have an uncanny ability to tilt bargains in their favor. I tried to warn you."

My partner spent the next fifteen minutes scheming how he was going to get his gold back, until I convinced him to quit while we were ahead.

"I guess the only mystery left is how we ended up in the cell," he said.

"Well, we did everything else to ourselves. Why not locking ourselves up?"

James considered that for a minute. "You know, I have a theory. You pulled off the polygamous marriage, right? And I put Franks's car on that butte. And judging from how our faces looked, we dueled to a draw when we got back. So I'm thinking that instead of a second tie-breaker, we teamed up and channeled what was left of that competitive kick from the tacote into another challenge. Your ward."

"Maybe," I allowed.

"You claimed our combined powers couldn't bust out of it, right? So I'm thinking that's *exactly* what we tried to do."

The fact was we'd never know. But because it was better than anything I could come up with, I nodded. "Kudos to us, then. Only took a couple hours, but we triumphed. We even got around to solving the case eventually."

"Amen." James smiled and raised his beer bottle. "Here's to a Grimstone adventure we'll never forget."

"Too late," I laughed, "but I'll drink to it anyway."

He stopped suddenly, his eyes going wide.

"What's wrong?" I asked.

"I finally remembered the name of that movie that's been bugging me!"

Before he could reveal it, a sharp rap sounded from the other side of the trailer. Someone was at his front door. I followed James through the house, while Annie sprinted ahead, barking. As soon as she reached the door, though, she backed off, tail tucked, and scampered off to her doggie bed.

Marge, James mouthed at me before opening the door.

Sure enough, the sheriff was standing under the single porch light in a flannel shirt, her official star on the breast pocket, a laptop bag hanging from her shoulder.

"Hey there!" James said, feigning surprise. "You coming to chill with the boys?"

"I understand Croft's leaving tomorrow, and I have something for you both."

I relaxed my guard, but only slightly. Marge didn't strike me as a gift-giver. We went into the kitchen, where she declined James's offer of a beer. At the table, James and I took the chairs opposite her.

"I've been so danged busy since getting back," she said, "there are some things I never got around to until this week."

"Like our official commendations?" James joked.

"Did you know we've been testing out a new body camera unit?"

I jerked upright in my chair as if someone had cattle-prodded my tailbone. "Yeah?"

"They're Centurion made. Smaller, less obtrusive. You slip the lens right through a buttonhole so it films everything from here." She tapped the top of her sternum. "It's made to look just like a button, in fact."

"Cool," James said.

Craaaap, I thought.

Marge drew the laptop from her bag and set it on the table. "I don't know if Deputy Franks's unit was defective, or it was reacting to your magical *auras*, 'cause it kept turning off and on. But it grabbed enough. Now would either of you care to explain what in jumping Jehoshaphat I just watched?"

"Look, Sheriff," I sighed. "It was my fault. We hit a dead end with the case, so I convinced James to take a special hallucinogen to open us up to new info. That's how we got the name of the anonymous caller. But we also blacked out, did a lot of stupid shit—including losing Franks—and then spent the next day trying to fix everything. That's why I lied in my message. I didn't want you to know how badly I'd screwed up or to take it out on James."

Her salty blue eyes cut to my partner. "Is that true?"

"Well, I was more involved than Croft is letting on—he's

being a standup dude—but yeah. Pretty much. Please don't hurl grenades at Franks or Rolls over this. We put those poor bastards through enough."

Marge studied us for several moments, then tapped the laptop.

"Is any of this crap gonna come back and bite me in the ass?"

"No," I said. "Miraculously, every problem we got into, we got back out of."

"With interest," James muttered, referring to his gold nugget. "And we also learned some valuable lessons. You see—"

"Can it," Marge interrupted. She returned the laptop to its bag. "No one has to know this exists, then."

"Just like that?" James asked, as surprised as me.

"I told you to work the case and have Franks ready. Technically, you delivered on both. Franks's testimony got us the decision, by the way. As long as you really did fix everything, I'm not gonna make a fuss—*this* time. Hell, I'm partly to blame for leaving you alone. Next time, I plan on being here."

I nodded, just relieved I hadn't forfeited my chance at a "next time."

Marge stood and started to shoulder her laptop bag, then stopped. "Before I delete this, do either of you want to see what happened while you were blacked out?"

When James looked over at me, I shook my head: absolutely not.

"Sheriff," he said, "I think we'd both just as soon move forward from this."

"Good. Because there was no camera."

Her confession took a moment for my brain to process. "Wait, what?"

"No, she didn't!" James exclaimed.

Marge's grin was positively cunning. "I knew something was up, and it didn't seem right putting the screws to my deputies. I knew it wasn't their fault. So with the help of Mr. Decoy"—she patted her laptop bag—"you confirmed my suspicions and then some. One thing to keep in mind as we 'move forward from this,' as you say, is that I've been doing 'this' a lot longer than you two."

James released a puff of breath. "Evidently so."

We walked Marge to the front porch and exchanged goodnights. As she motored off, her truck's tail lights dwindling into the vast darkness, I felt a whole new level of respect for her. That probably went double for James.

He snorted and shook his head. "You up for another beer, Prof?"

I was already courting a morning hangover, and the flight home was going to be bad enough as it was. But looked at another way—perhaps the James Wesson way—what did I have to lose then?

"You know it, partner."

The End

But the series continues. Join Croft & Wesson in the trilogy finale, Grimstone Reckoning!

GRIMSTONE RECKONING
CROFT & WESSON 3

The end of an era

In the months since I started mentoring fellow wizard James Wesson, he's grown into an adept magic-user, less likely to shoot from the hip. We've also become good friends.

But when he fumbles what was to have been our final case together—deliberately, I suspect—we're back to square one, and just as an old enemy we'd figured for bleached bones returns from the dead ... with a haunting warning.

A blood-thirsty being is on the rise, resurrecting Old West outlaws. But who is this *El Diablo*? All evidence points to an eccentric billionaire whose estate lies just outside our jurisdictional reach. Worse, an old-school sheriff seems determined to keep it that way.

As menaces teeter into full-blown madness, I'm counting on James to ramp up his smarts and spell-casting. Success will mean the end of the Croft and Wesson era, but failure could condemn all of Grimstone to a hellish oblivion.

And that's a sunset ride this magic-toting duo can't abide.

AVAILABLE NOW!

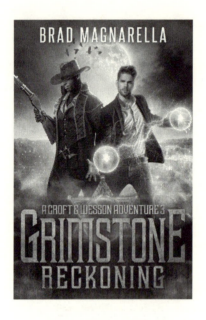

Grimstone Reckoning
(Croft & Wesson, Book 3)

AUTHOR'S NOTES

First, some context...

Croft & Wesson is a spinoff of my long-running *Prof Croft* series. It was written as a standalone, but if you're new to the world and want to read more, start with *Book of Souls: A Prof Croft Prequel Novella*.

That's where it all begins for Prof Croft. And it leads right into the main series, where he eventually meets fellow spell-slinger James Wesson.

Now for the notes...

I wrote the first book, *Grimstone*, five years ago as a contribution to a multi-author box set. At the time, it was simply called *Croft and Wesson*. I planned to continue their adventures as a series, but then other books got in the way (namely *Blue Wolf* and more *Prof Croft*s). This despite that I already had an idea for the follow-up: a Hangover-style romp. I jotted down some notes and filed them away.

Years passed, and I finally saw an opening to restart *Croft & Wesson*.

After the re-release of *Grimstone* in 2021, I went digging for my old notes to the follow-up. By some minor miracle I found them, looked them over, and decided the concept still worked. I did flirt with some other ideas, but none beat the original in the fun department. Plus, it would give me the chance to play with a wildly different plot structure. And so *Grimstone Hangover* came to be.

I'd like to believe my craft has improved in those ensuing five years, and that the 2022 version is an improvement over what the 2017 version would have been, but one never knows. What I do know is that it's been one of my favorite projects to work on to date. I hope you were as entertained in the reading as I was in the writing.

What's next for Croft & Wesson? You can find out in *Grimstone Reckoning*, which brings the wild trilogy of the spell-slinging duo to a singular conclusion!

I want to extend my thanks to Matt Abraham for organizing the *Eight in the Chamber* box set in which *Croft and Wesson* first appeared; to Deranged Doctor Design for another amazing cover design; to my beta and advanced readers, including Beverly Collie, Mark Denman, Linda Ash, Susie Johnson, Mark Mendez, Joy Ollier, and Christine Richmond, who all provided valuable feedback during the writing process; and to Sharlene Magnarella and Donna Rich for final proofing. Naturally, any errors or inelegance that remain are this author's alone.

To keep up with future releases, be sure to sign up to my newsletter. As a thank you, I'll also send you a pair of Prof

Croft ebook novellas, including a subscriber exclusive that tells the story of how Everson Croft met his talking cat.

That's all at bradmagnarella.com

I do hope you'll stick around.

Best wishes,
Brad Magnarella

CROFTVERSE CATALOGUE

PROF CROFT PREQUELS
Book of Souls

Siren Call

MAIN SERIES
Demon Moon

Blood Deal

Purge City

Death Mage

Black Luck

Power Game

Druid Bond

Night Rune

Shadow Duel

Shadow Deep

Godly Wars

Angel Doom

SPIN-OFFS
Croft & Tabby

Croft & Wesson

BLUE WOLF

Blue Curse

Blue Shadow

Blue Howl

Blue Venom

Blue Blood

Blue Storm

SPIN-OFF

Legion Files

For the entire chronology go to bradmagnarella.com

ABOUT THE AUTHOR

Brad Magnarella writes urban fantasy for the same reason most read it...

To explore worlds where magic crackles from fingertips, vampires and shifters walk city streets, cats talk (some excessively), and good prevails against all odds. It's shamelessly fun.

His two main series, Prof Croft and Blue Wolf, make up the growing Croftverse, with over a quarter-million books sold to date and an Independent Audiobook Award nomination.

Hopelessly nomadic, Brad can be found in a rented room overseas or hiking America's backcountry.

Or just go to www.bradmagnarella.com

Made in the USA
Columbia, SC
20 February 2024